THE TH

MW00948425

10/16/24

To Mary —

Thank you for your support.

With love,

Kathleen

Kathleen Brehony

Copyright @ 2024 Kathleen Brehony
All rights reserved
No part of this book may be reproduced or used in any manner without written permission of
the copyright owner except for the use of quotations in a book review.

Cover Design by Ann Glover annglover.com
Published by Triquetra Books www.thethirdactnovel.com

Legal Disclaimers

All rights reserved. No part of this book may be reproduced, distributed, or transmitted in any form or by any means, including photocopying, recording, or other electronic or mechanical methods, without the prior written permission of the publisher, except in the case of brief quotations embodied in critical reviews and certain other noncommercial uses permitted by copyright law. For permission requests, please contact the publisher.

This book is a work of fiction. Names, characters, places, and incidents are either the product of the author's imagination or used fictitiously. Any resemblance to actual persons, living or dead, or actual events is purely coincidental.

Ethical Considerations

The author has taken great care to ensure that all content within this book is respectful and sensitive to all individuals and groups. Any depiction of events, places, or individuals is intended to be fair and unbiased. Should any content be found to be offensive or misrepresentative, it is unintentional, and the author welcomes constructive feedback to address any concerns.

Compliance with Publishing Standards

This book has been produced in compliance with the highest standards of publishing. All editorial guidelines and ethical practices have been adhered to, ensuring that the content is accurate, well-researched, and presented in a professional manner.

The publisher has undertaken due diligence to verify all sources of information used in the creation of this book.

Author's Commitment

As the author of "The Third Act," I, Kathleen Brehony, am committed to delivering quality and integrity in my work. I strive to engage readers with compelling narratives while maintaining ethical standards in storytelling. I appreciate your support and welcome any feedback you may have.

Disclaimer:

This is a work of fiction. Unless otherwise indicated, all the names, characters, businesses, places, events and incidents in this book are either the product of the author's imagination or used in a fictitious manner. Any resemblance to actual persons, living or dead, or actual events is purely coincidental.

Synopsis

Shannon O'Connell is broken. She is sixty-five years old and looks twenty years younger - there's not much that makes her happy. Her partner of thirty years left her for a mutual friend offering only the cliché: "I love you, but I'm not in love with you." Her mother is disappearing before her eyes with dementia. And now, the death of her best friend - Linda - from metastatic breast cancer brings her to her knees. In this dark night of the soul - filled with endings -- she could not have predicted that this moment could be a beginning. The "Tribe," Linda's group of lifelong friends, gather at Shannon's family's beachside resort to celebrate her life as they have for countless celebrations over the years. And while Shannon finds comfort in their company, it is an old flame, the beautiful and sexy Elizabeth Matthews, who awakens something in her that was forgotten long ago. Can they overcome the emotional roadblocks they put in their own way? Will falling in love again make this Third Act the best one of all?

Table of Contents

Dedication

To my loving family and attached-at-the-heart friends – My Tribe.

To the sweet women – my lifelong friends – who read more iterations of a shitty first draft than anyone should ever have to and who always believed that I could write this book even when I didn't.

To Karen Jones – an amazing editor and an even better friend.

To Leslie Reeves – guru of MS Word formatting and BFF.

To my Literary Agent and dear friend Lisa Ross.

To Nora and Margot – good guides when you're lost.

To Shannon and Elizabeth who remind us that falling in love is always redemptive.

Saturday

Chapter One: Shannon O'Connell

I watch as the hospice nurse turns off the oxygen and takes apart the monitor that has shown Linda's vital signs in real time. Two things have been clear for several days: her death is inevitable, and it will come soon. The nurse – a professional and warm woman named Dorothy – turns her back to the Hudson family and me as she makes a quiet call on her cell. After six days of keeping this vigil, I almost missed the last time the blood pressure cuff inflated. I had become familiar with the timing of that rushing sound every twenty minutes during the day and every hour at night.

That predictable sound kept me grounded and distracted me from the brutal knowledge that my best friend is dying. I can't concentrate enough to read or watch TV. I can barely keep the rest of our friends informed through our group chat although I know everyone is counting on me to do that. I force myself to send an updated text at least once a day but mostly there is nothing to report. Everyone knows where this is headed, and it is just a matter of time.

Linda is dying in a hospital bed set up in her parents' living room. The room is sunny and opens onto a deck from which I can see the ocean. When the family decided that Linda would stay at home with hospice care, her father insisted that furniture be moved, so that the bed could be put in this room. "Linda loves the ocean," was all he said. We keep the sliders open to the deck with the hope that the salt air will be carried on a breeze, comfort her, and remind her of all the times she walked this beach and the amazing art it inspired.

The Third Act

Linda was a brilliant painter of natural landscapes but never took her inspiration from a photograph. All she needed was the memory of a particular wave or the movement of the sea oats when a strong northeast wind whipped across the Jersey shore to recreate it in oil on canvas.

From where I am sitting and sleeping in this recliner, I have a good vantage point to study the patient monitor. Dorothy had explained to me how to understand it: The top line shows heart rate, then respiration rate, temperature, oxygen saturation, and finally blood pressure. For the first few days most of those measurements remained relatively stable but things changed over the last couple of hours. I don't know how these medical realities might correlate with what Linda could be feeling because she has been comatose for the last day and a half. Dorothy says the coma is a result of her body shutting down and the high levels of morphine she is being given for pain. About twenty minutes ago and in unison, her temperature, blood pressure, and oxygen levels gradually decreased. And then, suddenly, the monitor sounded several loud beeps and the screen showed Linda's heartbeats becoming farther apart. In a matter of minutes, it is a flat line. Dorothy quickly turns down the sound which is jarring. We all know what has happened.

I walk over to the hospital bed and touch her hand. There is nothing left to do. Whatever words needed to be said to my good friend – like a sister – of thirty years had already been spoken. I stand there holding her hand for more than a few minutes hoping to see her take another breath, but nothing comes. Linda is gone.

Dorothy is efficient and quickly has the equipment unplugged and ready to be transported. The room, now freed from the familiar mechanical sounds of medical equipment, is silent except for the sobbing of Linda's mother and sister Emily. They are holding each other and weeping. "My baby girl, my sweet baby girl," Martha whispers. Bob goes over and puts his arms around his wife and daughter.

Dorothy approaches me quietly, "Shannon, I've signed the death certificate and Maxwell's will have transportation here in less than an hour. I've also alerted Med-Supply to pick up the bed and other equipment this afternoon. It is too hard on families to keep this stuff around for a second longer than necessary." Dorothy touches my arm. "I am so sorry. She was young. Sixty-four is so young these days."

"Yes, fuck cancer."

Dorothy nods in agreement a weary expression on her face. She has been an enormous comfort to all of us during the last six days, continually exuding both compassion and competence. She has steadied us, and the mellifluous rhythm of her Jamaican accent has been a contrast to all the tightness and grief that fills these rooms. I have no idea how day after day she – or anyone – can shepherd the dying and, at the same time, comfort grieving families. If there are angels about, she is surely one of them.

"You all need some sleep." She puts her arm around my shoulder. Dorothy has been the primary hospice nurse and we have become close during the past week. Death seems to have a way of doing that, strangers united under a shroud of suffering. "Hang in there," she says to me as she walks over to Linda's family. I hear her explain to them what she just told me about the funeral home and the removal of the medical equipment. She expresses her condolences and is out the door.

Until two weeks ago, no one expected that Linda would go downhill so fast. She fought Metastatic Breast Cancer for more than ten years and all of us were used to her being sick. Everyone sent lots of flowers, cards, texts, and visited when they could. In the last couple of years, we set up group Zoom meetings which we called our virtual cocktail hours. But, during the past year, Linda had become increasingly frail. She no longer wanted online meetings with our friends and resisted in-person visits by any of them. "I don't want them to remember me like this," she said. Two weeks ago, she told us that she was stopping her weekly chemo treatments that made her so sick, retching all the way home from the Cancer Treatment Center, then spending the next three days in bed too weak to even walk to the deck to get some sun.

"The chemo is all that is keeping me alive, but is it worth it?" Linda asked. "I think that I get two good days out of fourteen, Shan. I haven't been able to paint in more than a year. I don't have the energy to walk out on the deck, much less get to the beach. I feel sick all the time. I do not want to live like this anymore. I've tried three different clinical trials and they are not helping." We both knew what this meant. She burst into tears, and I held her. I was devastated but understood. Today is the inevitable conclusion of Linda's decision.

I open the slider and step out onto the deck. It is a warm morning for early September and the Labor Day weekend is just starting. Like every other summer, after Monday the crowds of tourists will thin down until the next wave shows up: retirees and couples with pre-school age children taking advantage of the lower rental rates and less crowded restaurants in the Fall.

The Hudson home is a comfortable beach cottage about four blocks from the ocean, and I can smell the salt air from here and the breeze feels good on my face. Even at this early hour, the beach is getting crowded with colorful umbrellas and elegant shibumi shades floating on the ocean breeze. These are early birds staking out their claim for the day. Past the rows of weathered beach cottages, I see the ocean and the water is exceptionally blue.

The doorbell rings and I walk back into the living room as two men wearing Maxwell's Funeral Home shirts enter with a gurney. In less than five minutes they have carefully – almost reverently – taken Linda's body out the front door and placed her in a hearse. Bob quietly closes the door behind them and motions for everyone to come into the den which is off the living room. He pours four glasses of Scotch – neat – and he delivers one each to Martha and Emily and then me. He gulps down the one he poured for himself and pours another.

When I drink alcohol, I mostly drink wine and Scotch is a rare choice for me, but today it seems exactly right. The sharp distinctive flavor that my Scotch-drinking friends have always called "an acquired taste" is lost on me and I find it more bitter than buttery or spicy. But I drink it because it seems right even if it is just eight o'clock on a Saturday morning.

The front door opens without a knock and Emily's husband Josh rushes in. He nods to me with a sad smile but heads right for Emily and embraces her. He looks like he has been crying. Emily seems relieved and comforted that he is finally here. Josh – an engineer on a US Navy nuclear submarine – was in the North Atlantic and the Red Cross Emergency Assistance team had to work miracles to get him here inside of a week.

Josh is a good guy and a strength for this family. He has always embraced Linda and all her Lesbian friends. When Emily started dating him, Linda said, "I hope this guy is not some military right-wing homophobic nutball." But her fears were unfounded and over the years he became one of her best friends – like a sweet younger brother.

"We have a lot in common," Josh once said to Linda. "You like girls and I like girls so we can agree on a great deal about life." Linda laughed and loved to tell the story to anyone who was meeting him for the first time.

Exhausted, I swallow the rest of my drink, and get up to leave.

"Want another Scotch or anything else, Shannon? We have the red wine you like." Bob asks.

"No thanks, I'm not used to getting my buzz on before noon." I joke and try to smile but fail.

"Shannon, thank you so much for being here," Martha says as she takes my hand. "Do stay, I'll make some breakfast. I don't think any of us have had a decent meal in the last week."

"Thank you but I feel the need to get home and make sure that Hedy and Molly are okay."

"Linda loved that puppy," Emily says.

"That was a mutual admiration society, for sure."

Throughout the last year, I often brought Molly over on visits with Linda. They would sit on the deck and that little dog would snuggle on Linda's lap. "There is nothing, I mean nothing, cuter in the entire world than a Golden Retriever puppy," she said while petting her and giving her a treat. Molly is almost a year-old now but still found a way to wrap her long legs around the chair and snuggle up to Linda.

"Get some rest, Shannon, we'll call you later and tell you what we learn about the next steps," Bob says as he hugs me. He is a strong bear-like man used to working with his hands as a carpenter. Even now in his mid-eighties, he looks like he could still do the job better than most.

I open the car door and am glad I turned down another drink. A week with almost no sleep and existing on pizza delivery or fried chicken brought by neighbors had seriously weakened me. It is not advisable for women over sixty to sleep in a recliner for almost a week eating pub food. It was a white lie to say that I wanted to make sure that my pets are okay. Hedy will be purring laid out in a sunbeam somewhere in my cottage. Molly has become something of a family dog who everyone loves, especially the kids. They frequently ask if she can have a sleepover with them. They are fine. I am not. What I need now is a swim in the ocean, a hot shower, and a night's sleep in my own bed with Molly and Hedy breathing quietly in their little beds on the floor.

I turn on the ignition and let the car run for a few minutes since it hasn't been moved in almost a week. I pull out my phone and find the group chat for our old friends called "Tribe."

She's gone is all that I write.

Chapter Two: Elizabeth Matthews

It's close to nine in the morning when I hear the chime on my phone alerting me that a text has arrived.

The message is from Shannon and one that all of us have been expecting for many days, but it is still a shock.

She's gone.

I grab a tissue and sit down on the bed, tears flowing "Shit," I whisper. I automatically start to look at the photos on my phone. I've kept a special album for Linda knowing that we will be looking for pictures for the celebration of her life that is already being planned. The only unknown has been the date of this gathering.

One of the first photos that I see is Linda in the middle of a night on the town during a Pride Week reunion in Richmond. She is dressed from head to toe in rainbow flags and holding a can of Miller Lite. This photo was taken about twenty years ago and a decade before she got sick. She was a lover of life, a superb artist, and a large part of the glue that has kept our group of friends together from the time we were in our thirties. Now here we are in our sixties and seventies. These kinds of friendships are rare and now we are entering the last part of our lives. I don't know where I would be without the strong support of these women.

I read the responses to Shannon's message on the chat and think that for a writer and journalist, Shannon has used an extreme economy of language in sending this news. I respond to her text to the group:

Heartbroken. Godspeed, Linda.

It was when they met in Richmond that Shannon first discovered that Linda's family lived on the same stretch of New Jersey shore where her family had a summer home. Their houses were only blocks apart but they didn't meet until they were in their thirties. They had to travel to Virginia to find each other. From the moment they knew of this connection, they became best friends and have been for over thirty years.

I know Shannon is devastated and I wish I was there to throw my arms around her. I would hold her until she is comforted. But, knowing her for a very long time, I am also aware that she will be the strong one over the course of the next few days. She won't shed a tear, at least not in front of anyone. As far as I know, she has not grieved for her mother who is being wrecked by Alzheimer's Disease. I don't know if she has cried or how she feels about the breakup with Kim because she won't talk about that. Her sister Megan seems to be the one who got all the Irish propensity for emotional expression.

I have been anticipating this news for days and so I am in Boston instead of London. My secretary is on holiday, but my good friend and colleague Susan helped me arrange some meetings that needed to happen though not necessarily at this time. But it was clear to all of us from what the hospice staff told Shannon that Linda would be unlikely to survive the weekend. I needed to be closer and able to get to the Jersey shore quickly. I check around the hotel room and tuck in the kite that I purchased for the kids and a few of the DVDs of a little movie that I put together to show at the Celebration of Life for Linda. I have already identified several flights that will take me directly from Boston Logan to Newark and scroll down the list on Expedia. I call Susan and put my phone on speaker, as I add a few things to my suitcase.

"I know when you make an actual phone call and not a text that it is something important," Susan says. "I assume that you've lost Linda."

I thought it would be easier to say these words aloud than it is, my voice catches in my throat. "Yes. This morning at around nine our time here."

"I am so sorry. I know she was such a good friend and for a long time."

"Thanks, Susan. I'm checking to see what flights have a seat. I will take the first available."

"I'm just watching the news and saw a story about the seashore in Florida. Jammed. Could be a busy travel day and long ride once you land. The rest of the world celebrates workers at the beginning of May but isn't this Labor Day weekend for you Yanks?"

I had completely forgotten that this is Labor Day weekend in the States. "Traffic to the beaches could be a nightmare."

"I will take care of everything here. Just go and be with your friends. I know this is a hard time for all of you. I'll text or call if anything urgent comes up. We've got weeks before shooting begins so I hope you can find peace and enjoy some time by the ocean. I envy you that. I can email you any revisions in the script if you want me to." I could hear Joe's voice in the background, "Joseph says he loves you and sends his condolences to you and your friends."

How lucky I am to have such good friends as Susan and Joe. Susan and I were hired during the same month at the BBC. She started as a bookkeeper, and I was hired at a low-level job in production. Thirty years later, I am a Senior Producer/Director and Susan is CFO. She is a terrific colleague, but an even better friend. And more like a sister to me than Melissa has ever been. Joe is a sweet man who owns an electrical company. Even after eighteen years together – a second marriage for both – he is still madly in love with Susan. She once shared that I reminded him of his sister who was killed in a car accident when she was twenty-four and that he is very fond of me.

The first available flight to Liberty Airport in Newark departs Logan in an hour and a half. I should be able to get there in time. I download the boarding pass, close the suitcase, then call for a Lyft. Standing in front of my hotel while waiting for the ride I text Susan one more time. *Heading out now.*

A text arrives back from her immediately:

S: Are you going to tell her this time? Or are you going to keep this crush going for another thirty years?

E: I'll have to read the room. You know. So, to speak.

S: You always say that. For the first time in a long time – maybe in forever – she's single and so are you. And at the same time…imagine that! You were once in love with her, and I know you still are. Coward!

E: She might not even remember.

S: Highly unlikely!

E: I have got to go; my ride is here.

S: Safe travels.

Traffic in Boston – just like driving in London – is always a nightmare but this driver takes a couple of frightening detours that result in making good time. I check my bag, find my gate in plenty of time, and after only a short wait walk the jetway to my seat in First Class. The disadvantage to having a job with lots of travel is that you miss important events like birthday parties, weddings, and just quiet weekends hanging out with friends. The advantage is that you accumulate so many frequent flyer miles that you always get an upgrade.

The flight attendant smiles at me and, without asking, offers me a flute of champagne. I must look like I need a drink. In another hour and half, I will be at Newark Airport, figure another hour to collect my bag and get to the god-forsaken area where the rental cars live. Then an hour and a half drive to the shore if the traffic is not too bad. It is only ninety miles from Liberty International to Long Beach Island but it can take anywhere from an hour and a half to several hours depending on the massive exodus from New York City and the populated northern towns of New Jersey to get to the salt air and wide beaches of the Jersey shore. If everything works to plan, I'll be at Shannon's by midafternoon.

I think about a conversation I had with Susan. A few weeks ago, she was, once again, reading me the riot act about my hesitation to talk to Shannon about what had happened in our past. "Everything about you screams confidence," she said.

"My sister Melissa would call it arrogance."

"Oh fuck Melissa. She's jealous of you and her church doesn't like you or any of your friends. Listen Elizabeth, you look like you're forty and a young forty at that. You run half-marathons and look like a freaking model. You have won award after international award. You are at the top of your game, and you are really acting like a pussy."

I can't believe Susan – with her proper British articulation was saying 'Fuck Melissa' and then calling me a pussy. Despite feeling so sad, I laughed. "What has gotten into you with all this trash talking?"

"Cursing always sounds so much more dignified when it comes with a British accent. Don't you think? The world has watched too much Downton Abbey, so anything takes on great importance even if we're just telling someone to sod off!"

Despite her colorful language, Susan is right that I am a coward when it comes to Shannon. Many of the documentaries that our team produces have focused on the environment and threats to it through climate change. I've interviewed Prime Ministers and Presidents often holding their feet to the fire about their country's policies that are killing our planet. Not once did I experience sweaty palms or nervous butterflies. But the thought of telling Shannon how I feel now and how I have felt for all these years causes me to struggle to find my voice. All I have to do is say, "Do you remember that night thirty years ago?" Susan is positive that Shannon will remember. That was a long time ago. We had a drunken encounter. That was all it was. Wasn't it? It did not end well. That morning after a night of making love, Shannon wanted to talk about what had just happened, but I shut her down. I had always been attracted to her and that night – even through the haze of Tequila – was extraordinary and not just because it was passionate but because I let her all the way into my heart. I couldn't tell her why this had to be the end. So, instead, I told her to go to grad school, not everyone gets into Princeton, and she left the next week.

Within a few weeks, she met and fell in love with a fellow graduate student. She and Kim were together thirty years until a year ago. I was as confused as the rest of the group when they broke up. No one saw that coming. I've tried multiple times and in every possible way to talk with her about how she is doing but she is closed up tighter than a drum. I called her sister Megan to see if there is anything that any of us can do to help but she is also at a loss. Susan is right about the current situation. We are both single and it is now or never. Susan is right, I am a coward.

It is thirty years later, and we are still surrounded by this amazing group of women. Shannon and I are still good friends and I love her, but that emotion has found a natural way of expression, an ease of being with her just as her friend though if I want more than that I will have to get the courage to say things I have held inside for a very long time. No matter what, I will not risk our friendship in the process. It is too important, too precious to me to jeopardize it.

The crew readies the cabin. They close the door and offer instructions about exits and seat belts. Without my asking, the flight attendant brings me another glass of champagne.

Before I put my cell in Airplane Mode for takeoff, I send a text to the group:

Leaving Boston. Wheels up.

Chapter Three: Shannon

It is still early Saturday morning, and the compound is quiet but then Molly comes running as I pull into the driveway and sits on the sidewalk as she has been trained to do. She is followed closely behind by my nephew Ryan. He is kind, handsome, and I love him like he is my own son. That often happens when a woman loves kids but doesn't have any of her own.

"Hey, Shan, Emily called, and we know that Linda died," he says in a low voice filled with pain.

"Yes, about an hour ago."

"I'm so sorry. We all loved her. She was such a good person, and you were so close." He puts his arms around me, his face close to my cheek, and I can feel his tears. He is just like his mother, I think. But I cherish him and his sensitive heart. Meanwhile, Molly is dancing around and whining for my attention.

"Hey Girl, I missed you," I say as I lean down to kiss her soft furry head.

"Mom and Dad took the kids to church and then they were going to swing by and see Nana. They picked Saturday Mass since tomorrow is going to be nuts around here with Labor Day on Monday and then Linda's celebration of life on Tuesday. The kids weren't up for church, but I believe ice cream is involved."

It is easy to see the love in his eyes when Ryan talks about his kids. Jack – not a nickname for John but just Jack – is the sweetest guy. He just turned nine and is eager to start the fourth grade on Tuesday. Patty is seven and a wild child who often says things that are outrageous. Ryan secretly refers to her as a badass. Her special wish for her last birthday was to be able to use a swear word for the day. When she told us the word that she most wanted to use was "Damn" everyone breathed a sigh of relief. No one wanted to be the culprit who could be blamed for modeling how to drop the F Bomb to a seven-year-old. The truth though is that everyone except my mother and, perhaps, Jack could be rightfully blamed.

"I'll let you go get settled. We're shorthanded today and it's kind of a cluster. I have to go to the grocery store since the veggie supplier shorted us, and I know it will be jamming this weekend. The Guinness order was ten kegs less than we ordered, and Judy is filling in for a bartender on the patio bar today. God love her."

Judy is Ryan's wife of twelve years. She is a nurse at the local medical center and is a Jill of all trades at O'Connell's. When your husband's family runs a particularly busy boutique hotel you learn to do everything. She has unclogged toilets, made beds, served as sous chef and reservationist all the while working full time and raising two kids. At Halloween last year Patty wanted both to go as Superwoman and so they did with matching costumes. Ryan hung the photo he took of them in the front lobby of the hotel. "If you see Judy roaming around, please remind her that we know she is Superwoman!"

I punch in the familiar numbers on the keypad and enter my cottage. Molly is still jumping and demanding attention. Hedy comes running from my bedroom, purring, I pick her up and snuggle her. "Okay, girls, you've got me now." I sit down for a few minutes just relishing the warmth of these beautiful pets, my most loyal companions. I am exhausted and if I do not get up now, I'm destined to fall asleep on this couch. So instead, I strip off my clothes and toss them in the washing machine and grab a clean tank top and some gym shorts folded on top of the dryer. I do not feel like looking for a bathing suit. I grab a tennis ball from Molly's overflowing basket of toys, and we head to the beach.

My cottage is ideally located on the property and only about a hundred yards from the ocean. I'm not sure if this will be a good thing in the future with sea levels rising but for right now it is convenient. For most of the year I can watch the sun rise from my bedroom window.

As we walk toward the ocean a few people sitting by the pool – regular guests – wave and call out to me and, mostly to Molly. I wave back. Except for Phillip and Rafael, I do not think that any of the regulars have any idea what has been going on.

O'Connell's Guest House is something of a misnomer for what is now a 60-room boutique hotel with a dozen cottages of assorted sizes scattered throughout the property. Over the years, it expanded to become a resort that includes two clay tennis courts, two hard courts, a good-sized pool, high-end restaurant, snack bar, a little store for incidentals, an indoor bar – modeled after an Irish pub – and another bar on the patio. But it started as O'Connell's Guest House and, my mother decided, that is the name it will always be.

My father, Michael O'Connell – a first generation Irish American – served in the second World War, came home, married Anna Mahon, then went to college on the GI Bill. They settled in Philadelphia where he rose through the ranks at Standard Insurance and retired as CEO. A family man, his greatest love was reserved for his wife and daughters Megan and me. He and Anna were savvy about investments, and they bought a large tract of land on Long Beach Island at the Jersey Shore just an hour from Philadelphia before the island was really starting to be developed. They found this ideal property on the beach that backed up to a lush maritime forest, and was just slightly south of Barnegat

Lighthouse State Park.

In that first year, they built a five-bedroom house that we always called a cottage. That house stands here today – though it has been through multiple renovations as the years went by - and it is where Ryan, Judy, and the kids live. Megan and Tom have a private entrance to their mother-in-law apartment on the back. Despite my father's heavy work schedule, we came to the shore every weekend during the year. Mom, Megan, and I would spend the summers here while my father worked in Philadelphia during the week and would come on weekends. "Family should always be first," he would say. He was a good man. After his retirement, my parents moved here permanently. Less than a year later, Dad died from a sudden, fatal heart attack.

Mom ran the place well into her eighties on her own with the help of staff. Three years ago, Megan took an early retirement from her job as Head Pharmacist at Mercy Hospital in Philadelphia and she and Tom moved to the shore to help with the business. They met in college and after their first date Megan announced, "I am going to marry Tom Kirk. I know this is love at first sight." They've been married for thirty-five years and still act like newlyweds so much so that after seeing some of their sweet hand-holding Ryan or Judy will flash them the "Get a room" signal. Tom still works as a financial planner from home with occasional travel to New York City or Philadelphia for client meetings and remains an active participant in the business.

The business is growing exponentially but In the past two years, Mom's memory has gotten worse. We needed more help and Ryan and Judy were quick to volunteer. Ryan was the principal of an elementary school in a high-income neighborhood in Philly, "I love the kids, but the parents make me want to pull my hair out." Judy was a Med-Surg nurse at a large, inner-city hospital. "I can find a job anywhere," Judy said as she supported Ryan and his shift in career. And she was right. She landed a nursing job before they were fully unpacked.

Ryan and Judy both wanted a change, and the growing family business needed them. The Ocean County schools are good, and the kids were excited to live at the beach and near their grandparents. Ryan has excellent computer skills and a natural inclination for marketing. He has helped O'Connell's raise the bar as a unique place to stay at the shore that welcomes a diversity of people and is exceptionally LGBTQ friendly. The large population centers in New Jersey, New York City, and Philadelphia provide a steady stream of happy, repeat customers.

My heart is filled with admiration and love for my family. We have worked so hard to create a place where everyone feels comfortable and respected. Even my tough Irish father – who could sometimes be harsh – always accepted my friends and me. Here, people are treated like family, and they remember, and they come back year after year. "A good business model but, more importantly, that is the right thing to do," my mother has always said.

Chemo was the only thing that had been keeping Linda alive and once she made her decision to stop, it was clear that she was going to die within weeks. Megan suggested that we hold back one of the three-bedroom cottages for the Tribe so everyone could stay here. "It's the least we can do for Linda," she said. And so, I sent a text two weeks ago that lodging was taken care of for the days we would be together whenever that would be. We need this. Need to comfort each other. Need to remember. Need to be together.

The beach is beautiful this morning – the water even bluer than it appeared from the Hudson's deck – that contradicts the sadness that began this day. There are only a few people here at this early hour on a Saturday morning: Three swimmers jumping the waves, two women racing on stand-up paddle boards, and a man casting a fishing rod, no doubt, hoping for a bite. By later in the day the beach will be buzzing with tourists enjoying Labor Day weekend – the unofficial end of summer.

Molly is spinning around on the sand until I throw the tennis ball into the water, and she eagerly complies with her part of the deal. She races into the water, snags the ball, runs back to the beach, and drops it at my feet. After a few tosses, she's had enough of the tennis ball game. I step into the water and Molly eagerly follows me. I dive through a wave and stay submerged until my lungs demand air. Molly is paddling next to me as I float. We are both buoyant in the water. I taste the salt on my lips and feel the sun on my face. Years ago, and just after my father died, my mother cross-stitched a quote by Isak Dinesen one of her favorite writers: "The cure for anything is salt water – sweat, tears, or the sea." Megan and Tom had that cross-stitch framed and hung it in the bar on the property along with other memorabilia, photos of family, some of the regular guests, and – this was Ryan's idea – the worst and most ridiculous reviews O'Connell's ever received on Yelp – printed out and framed.

I hope it's true about salt water being a cure for anything because it's all I've got right now. Molly swims back to the beach, shakes off, and we head to our cottage. Before going inside, we step into the enclosed outdoor shower; I hose off this sandy, salty dog. Molly hates water when it comes from a shower or a hose. But the ocean? Any dirty mud puddles? A dish filled with water? The pool at the center of the complex? Those are all good places to jump in water.

I throw my clothes on the shower floor and allow the water to cascade over my body, hoping that I can wash away some of this sadness. Let the water just rinse it away. I have been so sad for too long but that was not about to change today. Maybe I will never get back to who I used to be. I almost wished Kim was here, at least the Kim I knew before she left me. But that Kim is long gone, and I know that I must stop this self-pity, but I haven't figured out how to do it yet. I have a close family and friends who are attached to my heart. And they will start arriving soon. And that will help.

I remove the cotton robe I keep in this outdoor shower and wrap it around me. I towel off Molly, as much as she will let me, and we walk around to the front door of my cottage. I dry my hair with the robe and toss all the wet clothes into the washing machine along with everything I had in my bag from my stay at the Hudson's house. I put on an old Princeton sweatshirt and some soft cotton shorts, make a cup of tea, and sit down on the porch swing.

For the first time since I left Hudson's, I check my phone. There are dozens of text messages from the Tribe. Little emoticons of broken hearts, many messages of sadness. Marilyn had only written: *FUCK FUCK FUCK*. One of the first ones was from Elizabeth – *Leaving Boston. Wheels up.* What is she doing in Boston? I scroll back to dozens of messages from the Tribe over the past several days that I ignored or only halfway read. Three days ago, Elizabeth texted that she would be in Boston for meetings and so she would be able to get here as soon as possible after Linda passed. I find the flight-tracker website on my phone to see what flights left Boston about an hour ago. She should land by eleven-thirty. From lots of experience flying into Newark, I know it will take her an hour to get luggage and a rental car. Another two hours to drive from Newark Airport to LBI on a Labor Day weekend. She should be here by mid-afternoon. For the first time in many weeks, I smile.

Chapter Four: Elizabeth

"Dammit," I say out loud as I start the rental car. My flight left Boston and arrived on time in Newark. And then we sat on the tarmac for almost an hour waiting for an available gate. Then, of course, United lost my luggage. "God, I hate these New York City airports, and Liberty is the worst."

"Looks like your luggage went to O'Hare," the United representative – who looks to be about twelve years old – tells me at the baggage office after I watched the carousel go round and round with no sign of my suitcase. I am tired, stressed, and sad. I'm ready to blow but know it is not this guy's fault. "I'll get the address where you're staying, and we will have it for you by this afternoon or tomorrow at the latest. It's not really lost because we know where it is." I don't want to strain the minor point of what exactly constitutes lost luggage at United Airlines.

I am running at least an hour later than expected and there is still a ninety-minute drive down the Garden State Parkway to get to the Jersey Shore. I will be fine once I get away from this airport which is a complete shitshow of high-speed highways winding around and over each other. It is easier if the driver has a navigator who can scream, "You just missed the exit!!!"

My luck must have changed because I rather easily find my way through that mess of roads to the Garden State Parkway and go on autopilot. Over the years the whole group has visited Shannon often. Her family has always been generous and provided cottages and rooms for important gatherings like when Shannon won the National Book Award three years ago and every year for the

November Friendsgiving celebrations near but not on the "real" Thanksgiving.

There is something about being close to the ocean that is healing. I knew this when I attended High School in Richmond and lived only two hours from Virginia Beach. I remember the excitement I felt as we turned onto Atlantic Avenue, and I glimpsed the ocean as we passed high rise hotels enroute to a small mom and pop inn owned by one of my father's business associates. Those short vacations were about the only time there was peace in our family. I had never been to the Jersey shore until I met Shannon. She'd invited our group of friends to stay at their cottage court that is now something of a phenomenal boutique hotel and resort.

My heart rate increases as I cross the bridge onto Long Beach Island – or as the locals call it LBI. The barrier island is eighteen miles long and O'Connell's Guest House is at the northernmost end.

LBI suffered a great deal of damage from Superstorm Sandy in 2012, but thankfully the northern part suffered less destruction than coastal towns farther south. I talked with Shannon on the very evening that Sandy was bearing down and expected to make landfall. In all the years I have known her, this was, perhaps, the first time, I ever heard real fear in her voice. Shortly after that, phone service, electricity, and all communication were cut off for more than two weeks.

Before I know it, I am pulling into the driveway of O'Connell's. A cute young valet parking guy comes out.

"Airline lost my luggage."

"Fly into Newark?" he asks knowingly. I nod.

"I'll get you a gift bag that we have for the luggage-less. You know, toothbrush, toothpaste, all the toiletries that went to some other state. Even some aspirin."

I smile. "Luggage-less I've learned a new word."

He takes my keys, gets behind the wheel, and the car disappears around the building to the parking area.

I am happy to see Megan working at the front desk. "Elizabeth!" She rushes from behind the counter, grabs me and envelops me in a warm hug. "It is so good to see you. We're all so sad and miserable and know the only cure – if you can even call it that – is for all of us to be together." I see that she is tearing up at the thought of why we are all gathering here.

Megan is two years older than Shannon, but they could be twins. Both beautiful women with hazel eyes that look green depending upon the color they are wearing. They both have auburn hair now streaked with a wash of gray. Shannon once had highlights put in her hair and realized it was a waste of time and money since it looked the same as the gray ones that nature was providing. The whole family is kind and generous. And funny. The notion that the Irish have a sense of humor is evident in the O'Connell family.

"It's so nice of you to take care of us, but I'd like to pay for it. I imagine that this time of year it's hard to come by rooms in a resort town. You could have rented out those cottages a hundred times over."

"Absolutely not! This is our contribution to celebrate Linda's life. Things will slow up a bit after Labor Day. We are on the cusp of that this weekend."

"I've got the rest of the girls in the three-bedroom cottage right next to Shannon's. Since you and Shannon are singles, you'll be staying in her guest room. I'll walk with you."

Susan's words flash in my memory: "Just ask her if she remembers that night thirty years ago." I push that idea away and replace it with a smile at the thought that we all still refer to each other as 'girls' given we're in our sixties and seventies. Megan is a grandmother as are many women our age. What is the right way to put that, 'Women of a certain age?' But the real focus of what Megan says is a wrinkle I had not planned for pushes through. Staying in Shannon's guest room isn't what I imagined. I expected to stay in a cottage with the rest of the group. I calm myself down by remembering that we have been friends for thirty years. We know how to be easy together. Everything will be fine, and we are here, after all, to say goodbye to Linda.

At that moment the parking valet guy – who I just learned is Tyler – walks in with the gift bag from the little store on the property.

"No luggage?" Megan asks. I nod. "I'll have Tyler bring your luggage when it's delivered. This happens all the time and they're usually pretty good about getting those here quickly."

"I guess that means you have no clothes either," She walks over to a shelf with colorful tee shirts and other promotional products for the Guest House. She looks at me, judges my size and pulls out a tee shirt and a pair of sweatpants. "I know you girls like lavender."

"You don't have to do that, Megan."

"Yes, I do, and you know why because at O'Connell's we treat guests like they are family, and you are not a guest anyway, you really are family. I'll take you over to Shannon's."

"Is she there?"

"No, we expected you earlier although most people who come here fly into New York and I don't know why we ever thought anyone would be on time.

Sometimes it helps to fly into Philadelphia but, then again, sometimes it's the same and often worse! Regardless, everyone who flies into either is almost always late. Shannon should be back anytime. Bob and Martha asked her to help with Linda's obituary."

Megan is so easy to be with. She wears her emotions on her sleeve and always has. I have known Megan for almost as long as I have known Shannon and the others. Shannon introduced all of us to her family years ago when we had a beach vacation here.

"How is Shannon doing? We're all shattered but she was the closest to Linda. I know she is heartbroken."

"You know Shannon. You probably know her better than anyone, Elizabeth. She's stoic. Sometimes I'm not sure she is from this emotional Irish family. She thinks any expression of sadness is self-pity, so she holds it all inside. Always has even when we were kids. It's worse now since Kim left her. I really think it broke something in her between that loss, Mom's Alzheimer's, and now Linda's death. Kind of a grim trifecta. It's a lot and she seems changed by it all. She keeps up a good face but, if you know her well – like you do – you'll see it."

"What do you mean?"

"Shannon has always had this sunny, optimistic disposition. Failure is not an option kind of world view. She is more jaded now. Maybe, even a little cynical and closed off. She and Kim had tons of friends in the city and after they broke up many of them tried to get her to go out, do things with them. Several, I think, may have had a romantic interest. But she turned them all down and from what you've told me, even her communication with you and the rest of the girls has been limited. She hasn't even talked to me about any of the details. She really is not herself."

As we walk towards Shannon's cottage, Megan points out some of the new amenities since my last visit. "We have totally reinvented the restaurant, expanded the Pub, and I can hardly wait for you to see what we've done to the pool. It's crazy and you have to watch what it does to believe it! When was the last time you were here?"

"I saw Shannon and Kim in the City a month or so before they broke up when we all went to Disney on Ice with Ryan and Judy and the kids. But I think I was here at LBI two years ago for Friendsgiving and then three years ago when Shannon won the National Book Award and you guys threw that big party for her. I remember that Jack was about six and Patty maybe four. I think I was hungover until they were ready to announce the following year's National Book Award!"

"Ha! That was some party."

Shannon's cottage looks like most of the others, beachy, weather worn cedar shakes that have turned gray from the sun and salt air. All the cottages have a front porch with comfortable chairs and small gardens of colorful flowers that line the walkway to them. All of them on this side of the compound are arranged to face the ocean. On Shannon's front porch there is a beautiful teak porch swing that is obviously new and has sparkling hardware attaching it to the roof of the porch. "Wow, that's gorgeous."

"Ryan and the grands made it for Shannon. Ryan saw one like it in a Williams-Sonoma catalogue for fifteen hundred dollars, said that was outrageous, and knew he could build one. He has my father's gift for woodworking and so does Patty."

"She is one funny kid."

"You think?! Shannon decided to move here after she and Kim split up. She's made so many changes that took about six months. We all wanted to give her a nice housewarming gift, so we installed this bootlegged Williams-Sonoma porch swing with a big ribbon on it."

I remember from the group text – about a year ago – when Shannon told us that she and Kim sold their house in Brooklyn. Shannon said that she was moving to the beach full time.

"Does she go into New York often?"

"No. She's not teaching anymore and says that writers really invented working remotely. She occasionally goes to the city, and when she does, she often takes the train up with Tom who sometimes has meetings there."

We arrive at the cottage door and Megan punches in numbers on the keypad while handing me a post-it note with the code written on it. "We don't use keys anymore. Too many people lose them in the ocean!"

The interior of this simple cottage is stunning. I haven't been here in a couple of years, and it is obvious that a great deal of renovation has taken place. Shannon has had walls knocked down creating one spacious great room out of the original living room, dining room, and kitchen. The new kitchen is sleek, modern, with commercial grade stainless-steel appliances. Bright white subway tiles back up crisp white beadboard cabinets. A large, deep rectangular apron front sink set off with a black faucet and controls ties in with the countertops that are smooth, shiny black concrete. A small white table with four chairs is set by the window that looks out over the compound. There is what appears to be a brand-new coffee/espresso maker on the counter. But it is the seven-burner Viking gas range that commands the room. From the exterior of this little coastal cottage, I would expect gingham ducks and crocheted toaster covers to be the kitchen motif, but this looks more like something on the Food

Network or a high-priced restaurant.

As Megan prepares to leave, Hedy Lamarr, Shannon's gray tabby, saunters in from the back of the cottage. She rubs against my ankles, and I pick her up and nuzzle her.

"I was so glad that Shannon got Hedy after the break up," I say.

"Hedy was one of only two things that she insisted on. Weren't you with Shannon when she found this old girl?"

"Yes. It was about eight years ago, and she wasn't an old girl then. In fact, she was the tiniest kitten I had ever seen. I was in the city for meetings, met Shannon at her office, and we were going to lunch near the university. It was a bitter cold day. Frigid temperature with wind gusting around those giant buildings as if they were rock canyons in the middle of Montana."

"Are you saying that it was cold?" Megan teases me for my hyperbole.

"Let me say it more simply. It was fucking cold."

"That's more like it!"

"This little kitten literally stepped out from behind a newspaper box and stood right in our path. Shannon picked her up and stuck her under her coat. We went to nearby businesses to see if anyone would claim her but no one did. She even put posters around campus, but no one ever came forward. Shannon took her home and that is the story of Hedy Lamarr."

I continue to stroke Hedy, who purrs, but seems unmoved by the tale of her rescue from the wilds of the big city. I do think she knows that she hit the lottery.

Megan continues to tell me about Shannon's breakup as she straightens some mail on the kitchen counter. "Despite so much anger and crazy emotions, she and Kim did pretty well in all the other things that come with a breakup. After thirty years together there were a lot of entanglements, but they were amicable about selling the house, separating finances, dividing up stuff. Shannon was adamant about only two things. She insisted that she would keep Hedy and the gorgeous wave painting of Linda's. She said Kim could have the rest."

"I've got to go but we'll see you later. I think most everyone will be in sometime later today or early tonight and the kitchen crew at the restaurant is going to serve a nice dinner. Make yourself at home." Megan turns to go and squeezes my shoulder, "It is so good to see you, Elizabeth."

As always, I am impressed with Megan's warmth and the whole family is just like that. Everything in this place reflects Shannon's personality. Classy and highly organized. Oak hardwood floors with tan area rugs emphasize the light in this room. A modern wood rectangular table with eight chairs welcomes friends. This table has always been in the cottage, I remember the many times we all sat around it drinking wine, playing killer games of dominos or scrabble, and talking long into the night. A cinnamon brown leather sofa and love seat are new – at least new to me – and an etagere holds a flat screen television, stereo equipment including a turntable, and stack of vinyl records. The room is both elegant and cozy if that is even possible. The only two pops of bright color are the remarkable painting of a wave showing Linda's distinctive style over the fireplace and a wicker basket containing Molly's collection of toys.

I go into the kitchen to get a glass of water and have a better look at that Viking range. On the counter is a note in Shannon's handwriting. I recognize it from the days before email and texting when we sent letters and postcards.

E – Please make yourself at home. I had to leave but back soon. You are welcome to anything that you would like! Water in the fridge. Whites in wine cooler. Reds in the rack right beside it.. Beer in fridge. Tea, coffee, or hard liquor in various cabinets. Snacks in pantry. If there is a picture of a cat or a dog on the box it is likely to be Hedy's or Molly's but help yourself if you so desire." S

I set Hedy down on the kitchen floor and remembered the night that Shannon, Kim, and I were thinking of names for this kitten.

"What about Amelia as in Earhart? Or Eleanor as in Roosevelt?" I asked.

"She doesn't seem like an Amelia or an Eleanor. I think she looks like a Hedy Lamarr."

And so that is how this sweet cat came to share her name with a woman Shannon has always admired because of her genius. She was the self-taught inventor of spread spectrum technology used in cell phones today and an award-winning actress – a real movie star – who was the first to do an extremely racy love scene in a movie. It was 1933.

"You've got to love that," she said.

I take a bottle of water from the refrigerator and check out the rest of the cottage. One bedroom – the guest room – is freshly made up with a Queen size bed covered by a cream-colored duvet. A comfortable chair with a small table and a reading lamp is in the corner and a dresser with a mirror on the other wall. Two windows are open – the day is mild, and a slight breeze moves the curtains. A vase with fresh flowers is placed on the nightstand. I don't know much about flowers, but these are from the small garden I saw at the front of Shannon's cottage. The bed looks inviting, and I suddenly realize just how exhausted I am from the travel and weeks of fitful sleep worrying and crying about Linda's impending death.

A bathroom connects the guest room with Shannon's office which contains a futon, desk, computer, printer, bookshelves on every wall except where there are windows. I recognize the statuette – the reward for winning a National Book Award – that is hidden behind a family picture. I pick up the photograph. This was recent – since the kids look to be close to the ages they are now. And there's Molly as a tiny puppy. So, this must have been taken about a year ago. Shannon is standing next to her mother, Kim is nowhere to be seen, Shannon looks sad. I know her normal smile – have known it for thirty years – and this is not it. Other photographs are scattered on the bookshelf, there are some of her mother and father when they were younger. Others show Jack and Patty, Hedy, Molly, Ryan and Judy, Megan and Tom, a group shot of the Tribe when we all came for a book signing party but except for the family photo taken last year this is the only photo that includes Shannon.

Among many things I like about her, I have always admired Shannon's intelligence, dry humor, and talent as a writer. Her bookshelves are filled with an eclectic selection of philosophy, metaphysics, history, literary fiction, women's literature, and lesbian pulp fiction from the 1950's. One shelf contains a half dozen copies of her book that – three years ago – won the National Book Award: Written Out of History: Women who changed the course of America. It is a brilliant description of women we should know about but don't. Women like Sybil Ludington, sixteen years old, who rode her horse forty miles – twice the distance by Paul Revere – to warn the Patriot Militia of the approaching British Army. Women like Elizabeth Van Lew an abolitionist who ran an extensive spy ring for President Lincoln and the Union in Richmond during the Civil War. She operated this for years right under the noses of Generals and troops in the Capital of the Confederacy. She spent her fortune and risked her life to help save the Union and end slavery.

I vividly remember being in Richmond when we all first met, and Shannon learned about Van Lew quite by accident. She was working as a reporter for the Richmond Times-Dispatch and completing a boring assignment about a zoning issue with Shockoe Hill Cemetery. While gathering information for the story, she came upon Van Lew's grave and started investigating. She was fascinated by her life. "Why have I never heard of this woman? I'm astonished!" she said to her editor. "I went to William and Mary, the second oldest college in the country. The entire campus and all of Williamsburg is crammed with history, devoted to history. The college is fifty miles from Richmond…and we never learned about her?"

The editor – a hard-nosed newspaperman named Bill Cooley – told her she could follow up on the story but only after finishing the zoning one. "He let me do it to shut me up," Shannon told me. Quite to the surprise of Bill Cooley, her series about Elizabeth Van Lew was very well received and won a Pulitzer Prize for the newspaper. That column also spurred her to want to study history. Less than a year later she was accepted into the Ph.D. program at Princeton.

I pick up a copy of her book and turn to the back cover which is a great photo of her taken just a few years ago. Shannon is a beautiful woman with sparkling eyes, shoulder length hair that still shows auburn highlights. Her demeanor – up until recently – is almost a little impish, like someone just on the edge of laughter. A long time ago her mother told me that even as a little girl Shannon's eyes twinkled with irrepressible mischief. Her father said she was always up to some shenanigans. I run my fingers over the photo and know just how much I care about her and want to help her retrieve that smile.

The largest bedroom has a king size brass bed topped with a multicolored quilt. Two pet beds are under the window, and I remember the photo that Shannon had texted to all of us shortly after Molly came to live with her. Here is Hedy stretched out – larger than life – in the dog bed while the much larger Molly is squeezed into the tiny cat bed. "Now," she had written, "they just sleep curled up together in either one!"

The windows are open, and I see the ocean and smell the salt air. A little breeze has kicked up and the curtains blow gently. The attached bathroom is obviously part of the renovations with a modern gigantic shower with multiple showerheads, glass bricks on one end, and unique tilework the colors of the ocean: Azure blue, turquoise, deep green. It's exquisite but my attention turns back to the bed, and I can picture how it might be to make love to Shannon right here with the sound of the ocean and the curtains blowing just as they are now. I start thinking about all the ways I want to love her and how I already know how she will respond to my touch.

"Get a grip," I say out loud. I am thinking that all this is fantasy. We have been nothing but friends for thirty years. She probably doesn't even remember that night so many years ago and, if she does, it must not have meant very much to her. But then I also know how I basically sent her away that next morning when she wanted to talk about what happened between us. Go to Princeton, I told her. It was just all physical for me. And we had a bottle of Tequila between us. And, yes, it was great but that's not love, Shannon.

Shannon's note said to take what I wanted and right now – besides Shannon – I want a shower and a drink. Fresh towels are in the hall bathroom, and I wash away the long hours of travel and the lost baggage and Linda's death. Refreshed, I step out of the shower, dry off, and check out the new clothes that Megan has given me. The gift bag that Tyler gave me is a small velvet sack with a drawstring. It is printed with the O'Connell Guest House logo and the words: "Ouch! Sorry about your luggage, maybe this will help!" I open it and find a travel size toothbrush and toothpaste which I use. I don't need the miniature soap and shampoo since there was some in the shower. I think I will keep this and put it in my backpack or purse for the next time United Airlines sends my luggage to the wrong city. Not every establishment is as thoughtful as O'Connell's.

I put on sweatpants and a tee shirt. I'm clean I but look like the Lavender Menace.

I walk to the kitchen, open a bottle of red wine, and pour myself a glass. What time is it? I look at my phone, it is 2:30. That's not terrible and it's five o'clock somewhere, I think. And these are extraordinary circumstances, after all.

The door opens and Shannon walks in. "Elizabeth." Her eyes lock on to me and I feel a little odd being dressed head to toe in lavender O'Connell's gear.

Shannon looks at what I am wearing and smiles. "Luggage lost?"

She hugs me, pulls me close and to a casual observer, this embrace appears to be nothing more than a friendly hug between two good friends who are grieving, but there is unbroken eye contact, and it lasts just a little too long.

Chapter Five: Shannon

I am the first to pull away from Elizabeth's embrace when I hear the clatter on the front porch. The kids are bringing Molly home. I catch my breath and feel the power of Elizabeth's touch and the gaze we exchange is potent. She is a beautiful woman with eyes the color of the sky and I could have stayed there for the rest of the day. We both know what has just happened. Or at least I think so. But I am confused. I have always been aware of my attraction to her. I consider it a thirty-year crush but one that has always taken a back seat to my relationship with Kim. I don't know whether this newfound freedom is behind my reaction to her body next to mine or whether my heart is just so broken open right now that I am looking for comfort wherever I can find it. I only know that I felt the power of that contact throughout my body, and it was electric.

The door opens and Jack, Patty, and Molly burst into the room. Molly heads directly for Elizabeth – the new and unknown human in the room. She wags her tail and circles around until Elizabeth reaches over to pet her head. Molly likes her though, honestly, Molly likes everyone.

Patty hands me some flowers that I know she has just picked from my garden on the way into my cottage. "Mom said that you are sad and we're sad, too. We know that Linda went to Heaven and that you miss her."

Jack looks at me and runs into my arms. He is tearful – just like his grandmother and father – easy with emotions. "Gramps and Gram let us light candles at the church, and we all said a Hail Mary for Linda. I'm sorry Aunt

Shan. I know she was your good friend."

The kids suddenly realize that Elizabeth is there on the couch and charge her. She's been part of their lives since they were born. "ELIZABETH!" yells Patty at the top of her lungs. Jack – always a little less hyper than his sister – slides in next to Elizabeth and hugs her. Hedy comes running from the back of the house and leaps into Jack's lap where he snuggles and kisses her.

Jack and Patty ask Elizabeth all kinds of questions about London, how big was the plane she flew in on, can she stay for a long time. They ask if she thinks we can all go back to Disney on Ice this year and they tell her about the things that they are teaching Molly. They want to know what she thinks of Molly since this is the first time they have met.

I think about the last time Elizabeth and I were together and not just chatting by text or phone. It was a little over a year ago. Elizabeth managed to snag tickets to sold-out Disney on Ice when it was in the city and invited Ryan, Judy, and the kids along with Kim and me. My family took the train to Penn Station then a taxi to our brownstone in Brooklyn. Jack wanted tacos, so we ate at the new Mexican restaurant just down the street, took the subway, and walked eight blocks to the Barclay Center. Elizabeth had each kid by a hand, and they were jabbering about why Donald Duck wears a shirt but not pants and why Mickey Mouse wears pants but no shirt. I was certain that Patty initiated this conversation. Elizabeth turned her head backwards toward Kim and me and laughed.

During the performance Elizabeth sat between Jack and Patty sharing popcorn and the three were thick as thieves talking about how hot it must be inside those giant fur heads. Ryan and Judy and I were into it, but Kim seemed distracted and, although she knows my family well and is usually easy and friendly with them, she was not her normal animated self. She had been complaining about problems at the office, was stressed out, and was working late several nights a week. At least twice I saw her looking at her phone. "Everything okay, Babe?" I asked her. She nodded and smiled.

A month later she told me she was leaving me.

At the time I wondered what business had brought Elizabeth to New York. Normally, she would expound on the projects she was working on – she loved making films and was always eager to tell me about them. "Did you fly here just to take us all to Disney on Ice?"

"It was sold out, Shannon. Every kid on the planet wanted a ticket." she smiled but would not confess.

My memory is interrupted by Elizabeth asking, "Shannon, are you okay?"

"Oh yeah. I'm sorry. Just tired."

"I know it must have been an exhausting day."

Always cued into the emotion around him, Jack says, "I'm sorry, Elizabeth, I know that you and Aunt Shan are sad,"

"I'm glad you are here to help us all cheer up," Patty adds as she plays with Molly's ears.

"Lots of friends are going to be here later today and you have known all of them since the time you were born. You saw most of them on Friendsgiving two years ago," I say.

"I call it Fakesgiving because it isn't even on the real Thanksgiving," Patty counters with a laugh. "Can Molly come for a sleepover? We have to start school in two days, and we want to talk to her about it."

"What does your mom say about that?"

"She says Molly is just like her other kid and she can sleep over whenever she wants to," Jack says.

"As long as it's okay with your mom and dad it's okay with me. Molly, do you want a sleepover tonight with Jack and Patty?"

Molly starts chasing her tail.

"That means yes," yells Patty, as she turns in circles just like Molly.

"Do you still have food and treats?"

"Yes, we have all of that and also toys."

"Okay then, Molly can have a sleepover with you."

I pet Molly on her head, "Be a good girl and listen to Jack and Patty."

Just as suddenly as they had erupted into the room, they hug both of us and walk to the door, waving as they go. Jack pokes his head back in, looks right at Elizabeth, and says softly: "I'm glad you're here, Elizabeth. Shannon needs a friend to make her happy again."

I go into the kitchen and return with two glasses of wine. "Let's get some air," I say, and we walk to the front porch, and sit on the swing. She asks if I want to talk about the day and Linda. I tell her briefly about the flat line and the scotch and that Josh finally arrived and the sadness that the Hudson family is feeling. We sit quietly listening to the sound of the ocean, both of us contemplating why we are all gathering here.

"I was one of the lucky ones," she says quietly.

"What do you mean?"

"I was diagnosed with Breast Cancer ten years ago just two months after Linda."

I'm stunned. "You what? Elizabeth, you had Breast Cancer and never told me or any of us?"

"There was really no reason. I was diagnosed at an extremely early stage. After the biopsy, the breast surgeon said that it was small, treatable, curable and the pathology report after the lumpectomy confirmed that."

I don't know whether I am grateful, pissed, or confused. Honestly, I think I am all three. I stare at her, not sure what to say except, "What the fuck, Elizabeth?"

"I'm sorry, Shannon. There was no need to get you, or anyone upset. The surgeon took out the cancer, I had clear margins and only needed four sessions of radiation. Since it was hormone receptor positive, I didn't have to do the hard-core chemo the kind where you get sick or lose your hair – like Linda had to endure. I took Tamoxifen for ten years – one pill a day and no side effects for me. I just finished that a month ago. At the beginning, I had mammograms every six months but now it is every year…just like everyone else in our age group. I'm fine."

"I still can't believe that you didn't tell me."

"The only ones who knew were Susan and Joe and I only told them because they took me to the hospital for the procedure. I didn't tell my family or anyone else. Linda had just been diagnosed with Stage IV cancer – metastatic – and the prognosis was grim. We all knew that. My situation was nothing to worry about."

"Are you completely okay now?"

"Yes. Except for a small scar on my left breast, it is nothing but a memory."

"Promise me you will never hold back anything like that from me again."

"Yes."

"Promise me."

"I promise."

Jack and Patty are on the lawn next to my cottage and throwing a frisbee that Molly is trying to catch, and it lands at the end of my porch. Elizabeth gets up and flies it right into Jack's hand. She is eager to get out of this conversation. "Woot!" he yells with a thumbs up. Then they turn and run towards the beach.

Elizabeth sits down on the porch swing a little closer to me and when she reaches for her wine glass her arm grazes my knee. The touch is accidental, subtle, barely perceptible but arousing because touch is the superstar of human senses. Every sense has an organ, but touch is everywhere. Skin exquisitely responds to four basic sensations: hot, cold, pain, and pressure. But only pressure has its own specialized receptors and it's why we can distinguish a slap from a caress. And touch is fickle. Armies of finely tuned receptors represent the lips, face, tongue, and fingers – especially the fingertips. Not so much for the small of the back, the nose, and the ankles. So why am I having such a strong physical response to that inadvertent touch to my knee by her arm?

I remember reading that premature babies in NICUs gain weight fifty times faster when they are touched and massaged than when they are not. Waitresses who lightly and unobtrusively touch diners on the hand or shoulder get bigger tips. I shared that with two of my graduate assistants who were working restaurant jobs, they tried it and swore that it worked. Human touch is sensitive enough that it can distinguish differences between surfaces that vary by just a single molecule.

While touch can be choosy, it is also friendly and plays well with other senses, especially sight. This is why long lingering gazes, with dilated pupils or quick fleeting glances paired with touch is such an aphrodisiac.

The sense of touch deteriorates with age – I'm in my mid-sixties – and it has been a long time since I have been touched or felt any kind of excitement from another woman. But what I just felt from that casual contact with Elizabeth's arm is stronger than reason tells me it should be.

I lean into her. "I'm glad you're here, Elizabeth."

Chapter Six: Elizabeth

I feel the moment that Shannon leans into me and I want to tell her everything, what I'm hoping for, what I want for my future, but the timing doesn't feel right. I'm scared about revealing my feelings at this point because I don't want her to freak out and destroy our friendship in the wake of my attraction. We will still need to process what happened all those years ago and I'm not sure that I'm ready to do that. But since I've been here there have been a couple of moments when her touch has felt less like a friend and more like a lover.

"Would you like some clothes that don't make you look like a grape?" Shannon says.

I nod and she leads me into her bedroom, opens a drawer in her dresser. "Do you want shorts? Nothing fancy is happening tonight."

"Sure."

Shannon pulls a pair of tan Bermuda shorts, and a black vee neck tee and offers them to me. "Okay?"

"Great."

"That is quite a shower Shannon,"

"Right? I had no intention of doing anything that elaborate but the woman working on the design stuff for the contractor showed me a picture of one like this. Because the shower is against an outside wall, she also thought glass bricks would let in some light while still offering privacy. She was right. When I get up early enough, the sunrise casts brilliant light right in here. They call it a two-person shower, but Megan says that those two people could be giants and still leave room for more. Ryan claims it is really a community shower that can take in all our relatives, a few of our favorite regulars, Molly, and another dog or two from the neighborhood. Look at this."

She grabs her phone off the dresser, sits on the bed, and pats it for me to sit next to her. She scrolls through texts until she finds the photo that Ryan had sent her right after the shower was installed. The tile is not in, and the photo looks like a construction site, but the basic outline and the glass panels are in place. Every single member of the family, the head bartender, the chef, several of the regulars, Jack, Patty holding Hedy, Molly, a little friend of Patty's with a cockatiel on her shoulder, and several construction workers are jammed into the shower, and they are all waving.

I told you it was a family shower! Please say hi to Linda and give her our love!

"That's hilarious," I say.

Shannon laughs and then her smile fades. "Ryan sent it in the middle of the construction about six months ago while I was over at Linda's. She was still able to laugh even though she was mostly so sick. Shannon's expression turns to sadness at the memory. "She did love getting all the texts from friends. It really did matter to her. I hope she knew just how much she was loved."

"I hope so and I believe that she did." Sitting this close to Shannon I see the exact moment when she chokes back tears. I want to tell her to let it go. Tell her that you can't hold all that pain and grief inside without getting sick in one way or another. I watch her almost literally shake off her feelings and then she changes the subject.

"I'm so glad that you are here now, Elizabeth. If you weren't in Boston, you would be 30,000 feet over the Atlantic right now and not in until quite late tonight."

"I am glad, too. Logan Airport is a much saner way to travel than the New York City ones but I'm going home via Newark Airport. I'll leave here on Wednesday, return the rental, train to the city, and stay there overnight, then fly out of Newark at the crack of dawn on Thursday morning. Susan is making reservations for me for a hotel in the city. It was a whole lot easier to keep that kind of schedule when I was thirty-five instead of sixty-five. I'll arrive home exhausted and whining for a couple of days."

Her phone chimes indicating a text has come in and I can hear the same thing from my phone which is on the nightstand in the guest room. A text from someone in the Tribe.

"ETA thirty to forty minutes. Can't wait to see everyone. Something has to help this broken heart. Caroline"

I go into the guest room and change into the clothes Shannon has given me. We're about the same size and they are a good fit.

I sit on the comfortable chair in the guest room, checking my email but, mostly, replaying the time with the kids. I am so happy to see them. They are great little humans and I'm glad that Jack is emotional and connected. I think the world conspires against boys and men to cover up that part of themselves. For the same reason I'm glad that Patty is confident, assertive, and full of herself. Even though roles have changed, the world still too often tries to remove that power from girls and women.

Mostly, I love to see Shannon with those two. She has an easy, natural way with them and a softness about her in these moments that would go unnoticed when she is in her role as former NYU Professor, New York Times best-selling author, winner of awards and accolades throughout her career. With this crew, she is just Aunt Shannon.

Saturday Afternoon

Chapter Seven: Shannon

Another text from Caroline, *"We're here."*

"Let's go and meet them at the hotel entrance," I say to Elizabeth.

"Yes. That's good."

We walk toward the front of the hotel where Tyler and one of his helpers are unloading what appears to be an enormous amount of luggage.

"Good God, Caroline," I say. "You are welcome to stay the rest of the year and I can see you packed for it."

Caroline laughs, Nadine give me a nod that says, "True, isn't it?"

"Do you need to freshen up or anything?"

"I just want to sit with you both, have a glass of wine, and cry my eyes out," Caroline says.

"We can manage that," I say as I hug her.

I tell Tyler that Megan has arranged for the Tribe to be in Cottage #4, the one right next to mine. He says that is what he understood, and they will get right on it.

Nadine hands him a generous tip and she and Elizabeth hug.

It is so good to see these women. Elizabeth and I have been friends with Caroline since we were in our early thirties. After many years of short-term relationships, it seems like Caroline may have finally landed on the love of her life. At least that is what she tells me. Nadine has been in the picture for the past seven years, but she fits right in as if this group was made for her. They were married in a big, splashy wedding in Paris six years ago. Of all the Tribe, Elizabeth has spent the most time with them because they live in Paris half the time and travel all over Europe for business and pleasure. The other half of the year they live in – I'll call it what it is – a 10–bedroom mansion on Long Island. When they are on this side of the ocean, Kim and I saw them a lot, including several weeklong vacations to Cape Cod and other places in New England and Canada. We especially loved visiting Montreal and Quebec where Nadine's native French got us around so much better than the rest of us could with our sorely limited high school foreign language requirement skills. There are only so many times you can get away with saying, "Hello my name is Shannon" or "I'm going to the library," even when you are not. They were both here for the book signing surprise party three years ago but that is the only time that I believe Nadine was here at the Guesthouse.

"When do you expect the Richmond crew?" Caroline asks.

"Megan said that everyone should be here by late afternoon so I guess it could be anytime now." We walk from the front of the hotel over to the patio bar where the regular bartender has now shown up. All the seating arrangements in this area are configured in circles. My mother always said that this shape was the best way to have a conversation because everyone can see each other. That's true but Megan and I always thought Mom picked circles because they are so distinctively Celtic. Stone circles are ubiquitous throughout Ireland, Scotland, and Britain, and you don't have to go to Stonehenge to see any. Just drive down any rural road and one will jump into your view. There are thousands of them, and experts are not quite sure about their meaning, though there has always been agreement that they served some purpose as a gathering place for rituals and ceremonies. I once read a poem by Irish poet John O'Donohue and he wrote that a blessing is a circle of light drawn around a person to protect, heal, and strengthen. I think we might all need that right now. I know that I do.

We sit in one of the largest areas because before much longer we will be adding the rest of the Tribe to our group.

As if on cue, I get a text from Cindy.

"Almost there. Tonya says about fifteen minutes."

"About fifteen minutes till the others arrive," I say.

"Time enough for a glass," Caroline says.

Sophie a new, young waitress comes and takes our drink order. Everyone is having wine of one type or another.

We are sipping our drinks when we hear Marilyn's familiar voice call out. "Girls!"

It is so good to see each of them. We haven't been together in over a year and that is too long a wait. I vow to myself that we will find ways of gathering more often. Especially now with Linda gone and life speeding by for the rest of us. I don't want to run out of time. Marilyn and Barbara and Tonya and Cindy all elected to stay in Richmond even after the rest of us had moved away. They have remained good friends for all these years and often travel together like today.

There is a flurry of hellos and hugs and more than a few tears after all, we are grieving and not just getting together for one of our famous parties. Within about ten minutes everyone has settled, and we all sit down. I do not know if anyone else noticed but I do that I step past two of our friends to find my spot next to Elizabeth. I am inclined to wonder if she observed this, and I can tell from the look she gives me that she certainly did. This is going to be an interesting few days.

It is now late afternoon and more guests and some locals looking for a quiet place to have a cocktail are beginning to fill the other seats here in the patio bar. I can also see some increased traffic into the Pub. Megan comes around the corner and says hello to us. She knows everyone quite well and they are all glad to see her.

"I see a lot of changes everywhere since the last time we were all here," Cindy says.

"Whew! We have Cindy. Tons and, I think, all good ones. We've totally renovated the restaurant and brought it from your average fried seafood place to a high-end, four-star establishment. I thought that Tom would need CPR when Ryan and I brought in the proposal for all the things we wanted to do. But so far it is going well. We rebranded it, renamed it since it never actually had a name. It was always just O'Connell's, now we are the ever-fancy Lighthouse Bistro with linen tablecloths, a sommelier, and an Executive Chef with incredible experience. Both creative and delightful young women, I might add. They are planning a special dinner with some notable wine pairings for you all on Monday evening."

Just then Phillip and Rafael approach our group with big hellos and lots of hugs. They have been regular guests here for over twenty years and during that time they have become good friends with the Tribe. Phillip is funny, full of himself, and dramatic but, then again, what do you expect from a Broadway choreographer who has been at his game longer than most of the actors and dancers he works with have been alive. Rafael was secreted out of Cuba as an infant, landed in Miami where he was raised by a distant aunt. He once told

Elizabeth that before his fourth birthday he knew he wanted to be a doctor and he has accomplished that. He is a well-respected pulmonologist on the faculty of Columbia University Medical School. As out there as Phillip is, Rafael is just as steady, sober, always ready to rein him in when necessary.

You could not imagine two people less likely to fall in love. There is a twelve-year age difference, they are from different backgrounds and cultures and yet, the clear affection and the enjoyment they show when they are together is catchy. In fact, they were married in a ceremony right here at O'Connell's on the day that it became legal for them to do so in New York. It was June 24, 2011.

"I don't care that it is a Friday. We're doing this before any of those fucks can try to take our rights away," Phillip announced. They were married by a Justice of the Peace in New York, but Phillip said, that didn't really count. Of course, it did since that was the legal part of the whole thing. "I want to get married at the shore!" They hopped a train out of the city and arrived before noon.

Within two days, Megan and my mother planned and implemented a ceremony and a reception. They roped Tom into getting his online minister's license so that he could conduct the marriage vows which he did admirably. He didn't have time to have all the minister-in-a-box gear delivered so, instead, he borrowed a priest's collar and black shirt from Father Jerry so he could look the part. Linda thought it was one of the best things she ever witnessed. Kim kind of shook her head. The rest of us were just so happy that these two men who had been together and loved each other could ordain their relationship in the way that they wanted to. All in all, it was a fabulous day with more than seventy people streaming in from the city.

"Your family seems to work together well, Megan," Nadine says. "As part of a family business I know first-hand that it is not always easy."

Megan laughs. "Shannon please tell Nadine about how the pub almost caused a divorce between Tom and me."

I smile as I think about that ongoing, let's call it a discussion, that went on for the better part of a year.

"Everyone agreed that we wanted to have an Irish pub or bar of some type on the property. That wasn't the controversy. There were also no disagreements that it would be named Sean's, but Megan had a vision that ours would be like the ones in Ireland."

"Pub means 'Public House' – a place where people and families get together for conversation and sometimes music. I wanted an old-fashioned community gathering place," Megan explains. "You know where families and friends come together, where strangers are welcomed and become part of the community. That's the kind of place that I was imagining."

"The family had a big discussion about whether they would put TVs in there. Megan said, "Are we a pub or a sports bar? "That's when Tom countered with, "If we want to have a single customer on a Sunday afternoon during football season, we better look like a sports bar. Ditto for basketball season. And then there are the Yankees with a hundred and sixty-two games a year. Not to mention The Masters, the US Open, and the Indianapolis 500."

"How do you argue with a guy who knows so much about sports?" Megan says.

"And making it fiscally responsible," Tonya adds.

"Shannon, as always the peacemaker in the family, helped us broker a deal,"

I tell my friends how we found a compromise. There are TVs in there and plenty of them, but they are not obvious, and they all retract so that, on most nights of the week there is conversation and music including a traditional Irish band that plays every Wednesday night during the season and packs the house.

Megan says, "We have local and regional people who play music almost every night. I book the acts, but Judy is getting the hang of it now and I hope by next year she can take it over. Because, you know, a full-time job as a nurse and raising two kids isn't enough! I hate to brag but I am personally responsible for converting Millennials, Gen Xers, Gen Y into loving Bonnie Raitt, James Taylor, Carole King, Joni Mitchell, Fleetwood Mac, anything Motown, and, of course, The Beatles. I'm sorry and I don't mean to be condescending, but our generation did have and continues to have the best music. I'm still working on Gen Z – they're a tough crowd. But the Baby Boomers were already on board and ready to rock n' roll."

"Sounds like an amazing musical program," Cindy says.

"Many cover bands but we do have a bunch of local musicians – quite talented – who play original music. And, of course, several times a year Jamie Elliott and her band stay here when they are playing nearby venues like Madison Square Garden or Wells Fargo Center in Philadelphia."

"I'd love to meet them," Nadine says, and she is clearly a fan of Jamie and her band.

"You are welcome to come and hang out. You'll see just how down to earth they are."

I am enjoying Megan's enthusiasm with the Tribe and, yet my attention is clearly directed to Elizabeth who has been rather quiet during the last few minutes. I catch her eye and she smiles at me.

Megan has ordered a round for the table. Sophie our waitress has taken note of what everyone is drinking. This is part of the training that my mother and Megan have always included for new employees. She is young and this is only her first season here, but she noticed what everyone is drinking and even that Barbara has ordered a Beck's Non-alcohol beer which is her favorite while almost everyone else is drinking wine. Ryan makes certain that the bar always has a variety of non-alcohol alternatives for beer as well as mocktails. Barbara has advised him about the brews that are great tasting and the ones that are so lame that it is preferable to order a glass of water. He really might not know quite as much about beer as he thinks he does unless it is Guinness.

We are still chatting when the new round appears. Elizabeth is the first to raise her glass, "To Linda," she says.

"To Linda," we say in unison.

And we are back in the moment as to why we are all here today.

"I almost don't know what to say," Tonya says. "I think I have been in denial about how fast everything was moving. It seemed like just a moment ago that we were all hoping that the chemo and the clinical trial just might buy Linda more time."

"She did everything she knew to do," Marilyn says.

"Shannon, you were close to her until the end. I know this must have been so hard. Are you all right?" Cindy asks.

I take a deep breath and am not sure how to answer that question. I am not okay, but I hope that someday I will be. I don't even try to answer Cindy's question and instead tell them the absolute truth about Linda.

"She was just so tired," I say. And with this, Elizabeth takes my hand, and the warmth of her touch offers a sweet comfort. This contact is nothing new and would not raise any eyebrows. We have always been touchy together as friends. The whole Tribe is that way. I am feeling this affection from Elizabeth…all that and more.

Chapter Eight: Elizabeth

It is not quite six o'clock when we are all back at the patio bar. Everyone has unpacked, settled in, showered, and some napped for an hour but most of us hung out on Shannon's porch. We have barely reassembled at the patio bar when Ryan and the kids – along with Molly - come by to say hello. They are followed by Phillip and Rafael who slide into the same seats they had earlier this afternoon.

"So, this is the famous Molly," Barbara says as she reaches out to pet her. None of the Tribe has met her but we all feel like we know her since Shannon is not the least bit shy about sending photos of her and Hedy in every possible puppy situation you can think of. Molly loves attention and goes from person to person looking for pets and sweet talk. She lingers with Phillip as he reaches into a pocket and pulls out a treat for her.

"How many people do you know who don't own dogs but have an account on Chewy dot com, so they get discounts on treats and toys?" He asks.

Molly eagerly but gently takes the offering from his fingertips. "Charlee Bear. Only three calories," he says to the group.

"You are the only one I know who has Chewy on speed dial, Phillip," Shannon says smiling at him.

I am completely aware that I am staring at her and so I divert my attention to the kids. They tell us that later they are going to watch a movie with their dad and Gramps and that Molly will watch with them since she is having a sleepover tonight. Shannon has told me that these movie nights with the kids are frequent

56

and the one they are most likely to pick is Air Bud, about a golden retriever who plays basketball. The film was released almost twenty years before Jack was born but it stars a dog that looks like Molly playing his favorite sport so, as Ryan has said to us earlier, "Here we go again!"

"Gosh you two have grown up so much," Marilyn says as she gives Jack a hug. "I saw a picture that you sent to May, and I couldn't believe just how tall – and handsome – you are, Jack."

You can almost see Jack sink into the ground. Embarrassed a bit, I would say. Patty taps everyone on the knee as a way of saying hello and then lands on my lap where I am hugging her.

"You know that May loves the letters and postcards you send her, Jack," Barbara says. Jack smiles shyly. "She is so sorry that she couldn't come today but she just started college two weeks ago and there is basketball practice every day."

She reaches into her jacket pocket and takes out two 5x7 photographs that show the UVA women's basketball team on one side and the season's schedule on the other. She hands one to Jack, leans across and gives the other to Patty. Patty is pleased with hers, but Jack looks like he has won the lottery.

"She is number 24," he says. "That's my favorite number."

"How is May doing?" I ask.

"She's amazing," Barbara tells us. "She qualified for an academic one but took a full ride basketball scholarship at UVA and she just started two weeks ago. It looks like she will get playing time – unusual for a freshman – but what she lacks in height, she makes up in skill and attitude."

"Oh yeah," Cindy says. "I might have had something to do with that!"

Years ago, Barbara and Marilyn more than anything wanted to have a child. Barbara went through three rounds of IVF at the Medical College of Virginia and then at the world-famous Jones Institute in Norfolk. At least once it seemed to work and she became pregnant, but she lost the baby in the first couple of weeks. They changed tactics to have the child they so desperately wanted and decided to adopt. After several years of one frustration after another they were successful in adopting an infant girl from China. They had to deny their relationship and, I think, may have lied about Barbara having been married and now widowed. But they were ultimately successful. Beautiful Mei-lin – who everyone calls May – is now eighteen and in her first year of college. Throughout her life with them Marilyn and Barbara have always been conscious of celebrating her Chinese heritage with her and we have had some fantastic gatherings for Chinese New Year and other important cultural events.

"You had everything to do with that, Cindy," says Marilyn. She looks at Nadine who doesn't know all this backstory. "Cindy played basketball in college, then in a European league, then assistant coach at VCU her old alma mater. She's been May's private basketball teacher since she was three years old."

"That's the best part of my basketball career: Watching that little girl's confidence grow and her skills become amazing. Coaching in college was the worst part where the pay was so miserly for staff of the women's team that I had to pick up several shifts a week bartending just to pay the rent."

"The best thing that ever happened to you," Tonya says with a wink. We all know, including Nadine, that Cindy met Tonya when she was working at Babes.

"Anyway, I adore May and I have always thought of her like my little goddaughter and although we may be short, we are freaking powerhouse Point Guards!"

Jack looks at Shannon and says, "Aunt Shan says she is going to take us to see May play basketball in Charlottesville, Virginia in March." Shannon nods her affirmation and Jack smiles.

Patty introjects, "We saw May on TV!"

"It was a pre-season game between UVA and Rutgers and May got some screen time, a 3-point shot with nothing but net, and two passes that the commentators called 'brilliant,' I might add," Shannon says.

Shannon has told me that Jack corresponds with postcards to May all the time and she writes back to him. He told her that he wants to use Snap Chat, but his parents won't let him until he is thirteen. Patty knows this and basically says that her parents are lame about that decision.

I remember when we were all here for Jack's Christening. Nine-year-old May held that little baby on her lap with her straight shiny black hair and sparkling dark eyes holding this blond, blue-eyed baby boy when she said, "I think he looks like me." We all agreed. "Just like you are twins," Shannon had said.

We think that Jack has a bit of a chosen family cousin crush on May because he seems to talk about her a lot. And we know he sends her several postcards or letters a month. I get it. I know what a crush feels like, and it is often hard to find ways to connect. Go for it, Jack, I think.

Ryan signals to the kids and they wave as they leave. Molly gives one lasting look at Phillip who gets up and gives her a treat, "All right, Molly!"

And that is the nature of our Tribe, these connections are as delicate but strong and tensile as a spider web. Our relationships are the backbone, the strong undercurrent of our strength and our sense of belongingness. Most of the group, like Shannon, have good luck with a family of origin that is loving and supportive though I know that Cindy lost both her parents when she was in her twenties and that Barbara was raised in foster homes. My life has been saved by these women. Unlike Shannon and the others, my biological family leaves a lot to be desired in terms of love and acceptance.

Sometimes I lose track of how important we are to each other as my life continues to be busy and filled with so many things but the underlying context, the attached at the heart strings holds steady even in – and maybe especially in – times like this one. Linda is the first from our innermost sanctum to die and so we are now on unfamiliar terrain and the sadness that surrounds us is palpable and sits just waiting for the right moment to express itself. Like right now.

"I was just thinking about when May came into our lives and Linda bought us books about how to speak Mandarin and we were all so completely terrible at it." Caroline is smiling but tears are running down her cheeks as she says this. "See, everything that we talk about or will talk about has an association to Linda."

Caroline looks at Nadine, "Sweetheart, I know you speak six languages fluently, but I simply am unable to tell you just how bad we were at learning to speak Chinese." Caroline is starting to cry harder but laughing in the middle of it. "Linda always said that neither of us can barely speak English and that it is a miracle that artists can communicate in any language that doesn't include pictures."

"Oh, I can believe you," Nadine says with a smile. Nadine's father is French, her mother Japanese. She is articulate in many languages while Caroline struggles with every one of them and, according to Linda, even English.

I lean toward Caroline and say, "Linda was important to all of us and for thirty years. She was such a part of this Tribe. Like you, I don't think that I have a single memory of being together that does not include her. The only way to go is through it. But we have each other and that makes it bearable. Almost." Caroline reaches over and squeezes my hand.

"And it is a good thing because I have concerns that I've never had before in my life now that I am almost seventy," Tonya says.

"I'm afraid of running out of time. There are still things I would like to accomplish, and I'd like to see how Jack and Patty turn out as adults," Shannon says.

I don't say it, but I am thinking that I would like to be around to see if I ever will find the kind of love that I have been looking for my whole life. I don't want to channel this discussion to that part of me. I am barely holding it together as it is.

"I want to make sure that we are here to make certain that May is well launched," Barbara adds. "I think that is probably an anxiety for all parents who were older when they had their kids."

"When I lived in Germany, I learned a word there that I had never heard before in English. Torschlusspanik." Tonya tells us that in olden days cities had walls around them for protection and city gates would be closed and locked at nightfall. Latecomers had no choice but to stay outside the walls and face whatever dangers were there.

"Literally, that word means, fear of a gate closing. But it can be interpreted as fear of time running out. Kind of like FOMO or the Fear of Missing Out. I have that."

"I think that something happens in our psyche when we know that we have lived longer than we are going to live. And by a long shot," Nadine adds.

There is an unexpected silence in our group as I think we are all remembering Linda and where we all are in our own lives.

Marilyn signals to our waitress, orders another round, and simply says: "Meryl Streep, Emma Thompson, Jodie Foster, Goldie Hawn, Helen Mirren, Angela Bassett, Sharon Stone, Diane Keaton, Susan Sarandon, Bonnie Raitt, Jane Seymour, and then, there is Cher."

We all stare at her. "What?" Barbara says and she is laughing.

Marilyn takes a sip of her wine. "I am trying to remind you that there are women – like us – who are in their sixties, seventies, and beyond who are still hot, sexy, vibrant, fun, active, and filled with life."

She is not wrong, I think. Maybe we need a shot at this point of view.

"I mean, really, I miss talking about picking up women at Babes since it has been replaced by conversations about who still has their gall bladder or what is the best long-term care insurance."

"You never picked up women at Babes," Tonya says. "I've known you since you moved to Richmond, and you were always smitten with Barbara."

Marilyn – as she so often does – brings us laughter and a chance at a different viewpoint. You can feel something of a pall lifted from the conversation. Almost without thinking I realize that I have my hand on Shannon's knee, squeeze it, and say, "It looks like Megan has something to say."

I don't know why I did that, but it was unnoticeable to everyone. As we have always known, we are a touchy-feely group of women. But Shannon noticed and she leans into me and smiles.

Megan approaches the group, "Ladies, we have a table for you inside."

We get up and slowly move toward the restaurant. I stay close to Shannon. I want to make sure that I will get a seat next to hers. But, of course, I do.

Chapter Nine: Shannon

Megan leads us to a large table in the restaurant and one with a wonderful view of the beach, which is now mostly empty, as the sun is starting to go down. Getting this restaurant up and running, rebranding it, changing everything from the silverware to the menu to the name has been rather exhausting for the family and the staff. This was the last big project spearheaded by my mother. She had a vision of what she wanted and was clear to the designers, the restaurant consultants, and to all of us. "I want a place that has a quiet elegance, a calmness, where people can enjoy breaking bread with one another and conversations that go beyond the ordinary."

"I'm not sure we can control what they talk about, Nana," Ryan said.

My mother laughed. "Nevertheless," she said. "We can set the stage for that but, and this is critical, there cannot be anything pretentious or snooty about it. Do you think we can manage that?"

By all appraisals we have achieved Mom's goal. Reviews give Lighthouse Bistro the highest marks and Tom especially keeps his finger on the pulse of how we are doing. "Let's just say, everyone's inheritance is pretty much tied up in whether this succeeds or fails. So, invite all your friends in. And all the time," he told me.

Elizabeth sits next to me, and I am glad about that. If it hadn't happened that way, I'm pretty sure that I would have made it come about. I have had several glasses of wine and besides feeling a little flushed, the attraction I have been feeling for her continues and, if anything, is stronger than it was earlier this afternoon when she first arrived.

The mood among us has lightened up considerably since we were at the patio bar. We have ordered off the menu and everything being served looks fantastic. Maybe we all needed food since everyone except Barbara has been day drinking since midafternoon.

I remember Barbara telling us about when she went into recovery. She told us that when she was pregnant, she stopped drinking alcohol immediately. "Like that very day," she said. She said she came to understand that she could stop for this potential child who she did not even know but couldn't do that for herself. "I realize that you all party hard but there are big differences. You all can stop. You don't drink alone until you are numb. You don't hide it. As far as I can tell you don't wake up not able recall what you said or did and then feel enormous guilt because you can't remember. You can say, enough when you've had enough. I never could." Everyone always supports Barbara in her sobriety, and she is resolute and steady, never criticizing any of us and never, ever becoming preachy. And this is the way we have rolled for more than twenty years. We are different in lots of ways but always connected by that spider web of affection, history, and belongingness.

We had a delicious dinner with lots of kudos. We had wine pairings individualized to what each of us had ordered. Megan insisted that dinner and the gratuity were on the house, but the Tribe took up a collection for an extra tip anyway. Cheryl and David – the wait staff that served us – must have thought today was their best workday ever. This is a generous crowd. It's now about nine o'clock, and still early except for all the traveling that has happened today and the shroud of grief that makes my body feel like it is weighed down. I once read that the word *Grief* is from Latin *Gravis* literally means to make heavy. I wonder if others feel this in the same way.

We lingered over coffee and dessert and then Tonya suggested going to the pub for a nightcap. There is immediate and universal agreement that this is a great idea.

Sean's Pub is probably my favorite place in the compound. Long before a restaurant – much less a high-end one – was envisioned, an Irish pub was part of the original vision for this complex.

Ours was modeled after a one called Kathleen's in County Limerick – where my paternal Grandmother was born. It is authentic in every way, Mom, Megan, Tom, Kim, and I went to Ireland where we visited so many pubs that I could barely tell them apart except I really didn't have to. There is a certain look that is fundamental to all of them. Dark wood floors, furniture, and accents, Kelly-green or rich brown paint on anything that is not wood. We added a massive display of various liquors and a giant mirror behind the bar that covers the length of it with the name "Sean's Public House" and underneath it *Cead Mile Failte* which is 'a hundred thousand welcomes' in gold letters and Gaelic Script. Ryan had a neon sign installed that says *Slainte* meaning 'to your health' but more often just "Cheers." He has it tricked out to flash and blink when he pushes a button under the counter.

Perhaps even more than all the rest of us Ryan loves this pub. He is so committed to making this an authentic place that he holds a two-hour training program for the bartenders about how to pour a glass of Guinness draft to get the head just right and he has them periodically demonstrate that they know what they are doing. First, he tells them to choose a twenty-ounce, tulip shaped pint glass, pull the tap toward them, release the beer at a forty-five degree angle until it fills the glass to the bottom edge of the tulip's bump (if you use a Guinness branded glass you can tell where that is by the harp logo), hold it level until it is three-quarters full, then wait a few minutes for the bubbles to settle before filling it to the top, then ask the customer to sip it right. Even Megan shakes her head at that level of authenticity and Tom said, "Son, this is lovely but fucked up. I assure you the bartenders are not going to wait for bubbles to settle when they are pressed into action. But you can pour your own Guinness to those specifications and, as always, enjoy!"

There are at least half a dozen Guinness signs on all the walls, a mirror for Jameson, and one for Smithwick that the liquor distributor has given us. These make for the look of an authentic Irish pub and they advertise their products to our customers. "Win-Win," Ryan says.

We have dozens of old Irish musical instruments on the walls, pipes, fiddles, whistles, flutes, banjo, a small harp, and a mandolin that she was told was part of an estate that my mother inherited from a great Aunt in County Galway. There actually was no estate. The mandolin was it, the entire estate, but it is a treasured part of O'Connell history now.

Several years ago, Megan commissioned an artist friend to draw the O'Connell coat of arms. He was able to do this based on historical records he found in Dublin and in several churches in County Kerry – the homeplace of the O'Connell clan – and it is mounted on the back wall in a dark frame. Green with white and silver signifying hope and loyalty in love with a dark brown deer or stag in the middle of that white field that represents peace and harmony. Three shamrocks designate perpetuity.

Finally, there is a corner with dozens of black and white photos of family and friends, especially regulars who have been coming here for years. More than a few signed photos showing Jamie Elliott and her bandmates clowning around with the Tribe. There is the cross-stitch that my mother had made of the Isak Dinesen quote and about half a dozen of the worst and most ridiculous and insane Yelp and TripAdvisor reviews Ryan could find. Printed out and framed:

"You didn't tell me there would be so much sand on the beach. We tracked it into our cottage, and it was even in the sheets at night…1 star."

"Someone should have explained that there are fish in the ocean. One frightened my daughter. But the food and service were excellent so…Food 10 Letting me know about fish 1 star."

Tom takes our online reviews seriously; Ryan likes to scan them to find more of these.

Everyone is sitting at the big table, some with Irish coffee others still sipping wine. I see that Elizabeth, Marilyn, and Nadine have ordered shots of Tequila and that there is an empty chair next to Elizabeth with a full shot on the table in front of it.

"Oh, watch out," I say as I sit down.

"This is a terrific pub, Shannon," Nadine says. "I've been to more than a few in Europe and this is utterly authentic for America."

"Thanks. It has become quite popular among the locals. People originally referred to it as Sean's Public House since that was the way Megan advertised it, then it became Sean's Pub, and now to most of the locals it is just Sean's. And everybody knows what you are talking about."

Marilyn gives the cue for all of us to take the shot which we do and, although I do like Tequila, this almost burns my throat and I think that maybe I could be reaching critical mass or stimulus overload and I know that I should go to bed but that is before Tony the bartender brings a bottle to the table and Nadine pours another shot for all of us.

I am watching Elizabeth and, normally, she is a moderate drinker. The last time I saw her even remotely buzzed was at the surprise party for my National

Book Award three years ago. There is a specific look she gets when she's had a little too much. She has a certain smile that is endearing, and then she giggles a little. She is close to that now; I can see it starting.

I'm not sure who initiated the idea of going to the beach for a dip in the ocean. I think maybe it was Cindy but suddenly, we are standing up, taking the Tequila, and shot glasses with us and heading to the beach.

We settle into the sand, most of us at this point have kicked off our shoes. It is a temperate night with a soft breeze and a moon that will be full in two days' time, so it is bright here at the oceanfront.

We start reminiscing about Linda and there are so many stories we might be here all night.

"One of my favorite tall tales about Linda was when she was dating that woman from Pittsburgh. What was her name?" Cindy asks.

"Kelly," I answer.

"Yes, Kelly. They weren't together all that long, but they really had a good time and lots of fun. They took pictures in front of various signs around the country that had suggestive names like Intercourse Pennsylvania which she told me used to be named "Cross Keys.""

"Who would change your town name from Cross Keys to Intercourse for God's sake?" said Barbara.

"Someone who wanted Linda and Kelly to come and take photos of themselves in front of their bawdy sign," Cindy says.

I remember Linda telling me that Kelly had a conference in Battle Creek, and they drove almost two hours out of their way to take their picture in front of the sign welcoming them to the town of Climax, Michigan.

"Linda admitted that this was a rather adolescent hobby even though they were not in their teens. Not even close. She said that she preferred to think of this as an esoteric pastime." I remind them.

"But, God, they had so many laughs doing this."

"Who would do that today?" Marilyn says, "But, now that I think of it, if we go home by Route 13 through the Eastern Shore in Accomack County, we can take a picture of all four of us in front of the Assawoman town sign."

Now I think that Tonya might fall out. "Who…Who…names their town Assawoman?"

"Wait," Marilyn says, "It gets worse. The town was originally named Assawaman which was bad enough but then in 1966 they intentionally changed it to Assawoman. On purpose!"

"How about the time that Linda wanted us all to have a reunion and go to a Rave at some disco bar in D.C.," Barbara says.

"I remember how we got ripped off by those cabbies!" Marilyn says.

It was the early 1990's and most of us had left Richmond but we all agreed to gather in Washington, D.C.. Linda had arranged for all of us to stay in a hotel near Dupont Circle which was expensive even in those days, so we piled into two rooms with a door adjoining. I have no idea how many people the management thought were staying there but we just kept asking the desk for more towels. She found this Brazilian restaurant where we all had dinner and, I am not a vegetarian, but this was like hanging out in a meat locker. We took two cabs to this bar – The DC11 – because it didn't even open until eleven PM. The cab rides were about thirty minutes long with the meters running as these guys proceeded convoy style. When we finally got out at the bar, Tonya looked down the street and said, "Isn't that the restaurant where we just ate like less than a block away?" It was.

"I'll be we didn't stay in the Rave for more than fifteen minutes," Shannon says.

"If that long," I add.

The pulsing lights, the pounding music that you could feel in your chest more than you could hear in your ears was overwhelming. We ended up in an all-night pancake house drinking tepid coffee and laughing about our big night out on the town.

"Linda did many wonderful things, but she was not always the best travel agent for planning events. Do you recall that time that she rented that party bus for her birthday and took us to every lesbian bar in Richmond?" Caroline asks.

"I do remember, and I can tell you exactly when it was because I had never even heard of a party bus before then. It was Linda's thirty-fifth birthday," Cindy remembers.

"The problem with a lesbian bar crawl of Richmond at that time was that there was only one bar – Babes! So, it was not much of a tour. We did stop by that awful little hole-in-the-wall at the edge of the Fan District that served overpriced warm beer and you felt like you might get mugged even while sitting at one of the tables. And those were the inside tables! Then we were back in that bus and just basically driving around Richmond for three hours," Tonya says.

"Linda was so excited because there was a dance pole in the middle of that vehicle. At our age now, we would use it as a grab bar, I'm sure," Barbara says, and we all laugh because it is true.

"That is so fucking true," Caroline says and she rarely if ever says 'fucking' but she did right now.

"God, she was so much fun. Such a lover of life. How about all those everyday parties when we would all be drinking wine at her house. Suddenly, and at the end of the evening, she would go upstairs and come down with half a dozen towels – the unofficial signal to head over to Maymont Park, jump in the fountain at the Italian Garden, and race away before anyone could call security on us. So uninhibited and easy with all of us. She was one in a million," Caroline remembers.

Normally, I am less disclosive about my feelings but between the alcohol, my broken heart, and holding back tears, I say, "I don't know what these next few weeks are going to be like without her. I can't even imagine how I will feel especially when we all separate and go back to our lives in a couple of days."

Elizabeth is sitting next to me and puts her arm around me. "We are all always here for you, Shannon. Come to London for a visit. We can go to that Anne Lister place in Halifax that your friend Amanda wrote about in her novel. It will take your mind off things even if only a little."

"Or Richmond," Barbara says.

"Or Paris," Caroline chimes in.

Marilyn says, "I'm taking London or Paris!"

"If Linda was here, she would have one more shot and jump into that water and skinny dip," Barbara says.

"God, how many times did she do that?" I ask.

"Plenty!" Tonya reminds us.

Nadine pours everyone another shot, cocks her head back, and swallows hers. "To Linda," she says loudly, and we all raise our glasses to toast to our friend.

With that Nadine strips off her shirt, drops her shorts. "To Linda," she yells as she races to the surf.

Like a starters gun at a track meet and right on cue, everyone begins taking off their clothes and running into the ocean.

"Oh fuck," I say to Elizabeth, "here we go." She just smiles as she throws her shirt on the sand and follows them into the ocean. Peer pressure? Who knows? Next thing I do is go in with the rest of them. I think that only Nadine is completely naked, the rest of us are wearing some combination of tank top or bra or underwear or shorts or something.

The water is cool but comfortable and I think that it is serving to sober me up a bit. I am diving through the water when a rogue wave knocks all of us down and I find myself holding on to Elizabeth as we are both swept toward the beach.

When we finally stop tumbling, I am on top of her as the water pours over us. We are lost in each other's eyes but just for a moment. Now everyone is up and making sure that we are all accounted for. I am the first one to get my bearings and stand. I offer my hand and help her up.

Back on the beach I can see that Megan has been here and left a pile of neatly folded and fresh towels. On the top is a carefully written note in her handwriting: *Please don't get us busted by the LBI Police Department. We're hosting their Christmas Party. Also, don't let anyone drown. Love you!*

Elizabeth smiles at me and I can't even imagine any other woman who attracts me and then draws me in with such enormous power.

Chapter Ten: Elizabeth

I rinsed off in the outdoor shower because I was covered with sand and salt water, but I don't even have the energy to do anything other than towel off my hair, throw on an oversized tee shirt that Shannon had given me, and go to bed. I should have listened to my instincts and refused that last shot toasting to Linda. I'll bet all of us were overserved – or overserved ourselves I should say – trying to shake the sadness that surrounds us. This bed is comfortable and between my exhaustion, Tequila, and wine, I should have fallen asleep an hour ago, but I'm distracted by all these passionate and immediate feelings about Shannon, sleeping just on the other side of this wall that separates these bedrooms.

I am struggling to understand why I was able to contain this powerful attraction to her for all these years, but I seem to be almost incapable of doing it now. Shortly after I moved to London, I felt close to Susan and shared with her just a little of my history with Shannon, my feelings about her, and my regrets that we never were able to take our relationship beyond a close friendship. She suggested that I speak with a particular Astrologer – who also seemed to be something of a channel. She said that he had helped Joe and her sort through some things early in their relationship.

"That might be a little too out there for me," I had told her.

She argued that I was being close-minded and might be missing a chance to better understand this complicated relationship with one of my best friends. Reluctantly, I made an appointment expecting to see him in some place with beaded curtains, Patchouli incense wafting through the air, and New Age music coming at me from all directions. Instead, I met him in a building in the Central Business District that was unremarkable and could have been the professional setting for any accountant or barrister. The nameplate on the door to his office simply had his name: George Thomasson. Nothing more. No reference to divination, planets, the ability to communicate beyond the veil to the other side, or whatever else he can do. Up to this point, he knew only my name and my birthdate.

He was a handsome, distinguished looking guy dressed in business casual clothes and maybe only a few years older than I was at the time. He welcomed me and offered water or tea. I thanked him and chose water. He then set out two bottles of Pellegrino on the coffee table between our chairs. He rustled through papers printed with what appeared to be my astrological chart. We started with my Sun Sign in Gemini, and he went on telling me about where my planets stand in the various astrological Houses. It's a lot of information and I am trying to keep up. Then he stopped and asked a simple question that produced a strong reaction from me.

"Do you love her?"

He has no idea about my history or even why I am here and so I don't have a clue as to where he is coming from, but I nodded affirmatively.

"What is her name and when is her birthday?"

I told him and he wrote some notes then walked over to the desk that held a number of books and a computer. He typed on the keyboard for a couple of minutes and then printed something which he put with his other papers and returned to the chair he had been sitting in.

He closed his eyes, and I can't tell if he is processing information that he just pulled off the printer or communicating with my past lives or some spirit guides but I'm anxious and eager to hear what he has to say.

He told me that there are many ways but specifically three critical ones in which my astrology and Shannon's overlap and connect. He made it clear that these were three symbols that showed up repeatedly.

"First," he said, "The two of you enjoy an Ease of Affection. Second, you both share a Duty to understand the true nature of this relationship. And third, there is huge energy for Physicality."

Then he explained that Ease of Affection has to do with general likability between us. Many shared values and world views mean that conflict is negligible and that, if there ever was a quarrel, it would most likely be resolved quickly and easily. In short, he emphasized, it's as simple as this: we genuinely like each other. We are happy when we spend time together. I know this to be true for us in every form of relationship we have ever had and for thirty years.

Second, and then he looked directly at me and said I had to honestly assess if there was any kind of Martyr/Savior complex going on in the relationship.

"What do you mean?"

"Does your friend Shannon offer some kind of escape from something in your life that is hard or untenable?" I nodded and admitted that, perhaps, all those years ago a relationship with Shannon may have been a way out of my unhealthy and sad – toxic really – relationship with Lauren. He cautioned me to be conscious and aware of my motivations.

Finally, he told me that the third symbol that was so obvious in our overlapping astrology was Physicality and that he meant that there would always be something physical between us. Sex? Perhaps, but not necessarily. Physical affection? Absolutely.

He leaned forward and in a cautionary but kindly tone said, "The reason that no one can predict the future with astrology, or any other practice of prophecy is because there is no part of destiny that does not include free will and no one but the individual herself can determine what those choices will be."

Then he sat back in his chair and closed his eyes while still talking to me. He emphasized again that there is – and always has been a lot of energy between Shannon and me. He said that this energy is like putting a saucepan filled with water on a red-hot stove. It will bubble and as it boils even harder, it can become unmanageable. Sometimes, he said, you need to pull it off the heat and let it simmer. He stressed how important it is to manage this energy. Not control it but manage it. When Shannon and I are in physical proximity, he said once again, there is enormous energy.

All of what he had said rang true for me. And I think that the Martyr/Savior complex might have been true all those years ago but I'm not sure how it could account for a thirty-year crush. Somehow, and likely because she was in a committed relationship with Kim, I have kept the saucepan off the burner, and it has been simmering – at least for me – for a long time. But ever since I arrived and even more so after the first touch in that hug, my saucepan was back to a full boil. Is it because we are both now single? Is it because we are grieving for the loss of Linda? I am only guessing as to whether Shannon is feeling anything like what I am. As friends, we have always touched each other with affection but there have been moments today that definitely felt sexual. I really can't tell if she is sending that signal to me or if my hopeful and utterly passionate emotions are creating massive projections about what is happening here. Is this real or is it only what I am wanting to be real?

I start thinking about a poem written by an Australian self-taught poet named Beau Taplin. I learned about him some years ago when I was in Sydney for several months working on a project and bought his book:

One day,

whether you are

14, 28, or 65

you will stumble upon

someone who will start.

a fire in you that cannot die.

However, the saddest,

most awful truth

you will ever come to find –

is they are not always

with whom we spend our lives.

When I first read this, it felt like a mantra about my regrets that I had not made different choices all those years ago. It sums up my feelings about my relationship with Shannon.

How could I have been so blind thirty years ago? How could I have made the choice – no matter how briefly – to stay with a woman who never really loved me and sacrifice what I knew very soon afterwards could have been something real that I have been looking for my whole life and without success.

We sat on her veranda on a Sunday afternoon and Susan wanted to know about my session with George Thomasson. I knew that to adequately explain what I had learned from him would require talking about some things that I had never revealed to anyone. I said that I would tell her about the night when I first began to understand my feelings about Shannon and that was thirty years ago. I told her that I had been quietly seeing a woman named Lauren for over a year. One day, out of the blue, she sent a voice mail telling me never to contact her again.

"Do you want the whole pathetic backstory?" I asked her.

"Absolutely, yes please!"

"There was no reason for Lauren to leave that message. Nothing had happened to cause this sudden change in her feelings and then there was no opportunity to even try to make sense of it. I tried several times to call her, but she never responded. The only way I could reach her was through her phone on campus. I called but the voice mailbox was full. I raced over to her faculty office and searched all around the Department then to the tv station but she wasn't there."

Even though this whole conversation was painful it was a relief to finally talk about it. I explained how Shannon had come by that evening, found me to be pitiful and just a little drunk, offered to hang out and keep me company. We had been good friends for more than a year and, despite my love for Lauren, I was always attracted to her. That night she was a comforting presence, like she always had been. She was there to listen but didn't press me to talk because I clearly wasn't ready to do that. We killed a bottle of Tequila, opened a second, and then one thing led to another, and we made love all night long and, maybe for the first time in my life I thought there might be something more than what I had ever experienced before.

"That sounds wonderful. So, what was the problem and who was this Lauren woman?"

"She was a popular newscaster and an adjunct professor at VCU. She was on my thesis committee so there were lots of opportunities for interaction. She was older than me and married to a man who was running for office. She told me that they were separated but still living together and that she had agreed to maintain the public illusion of a happy marriage because that was important to his political ambitions. But it turns out that wasn't quite true. We had seen each other for more than a year. And it was complicated for a bunch of reasons, not the least of which is that faculty aren't supposed to be sleeping with their students. No one knew, not even my best friends in the Tribe. No one."

Not unkindly but directly, Susan had said, "You really fell for that old con called we're separated but still living together and all that, did you?"

I nodded. "It made sense to keep everything secret. She and her husband were in the news every day. It was the mid-1980's and a very different climate. Not at all like today. We were the oldest group of lesbians who did anything publicly, like produce concerts and hold retreats and parties. We were only in our thirties and everyone older than us was, honestly, invisible. The women's music scene was in its infancy and homophobia was everywhere. Ellen, Randy Rainbow, Brandi Carlile and other out celebrities weren't even on anyone's radar. She would have been fired and I would have been tossed out of grad school. On top of that, I was naïve and maybe just a little stupid."

Susan smiled kindly and patted my knee. "It's easy to fall for those kinds of lies when you are feeling in love."

Then I revealed to Susan that I had been still so hung up on Lauren and so hurt by her that the next morning I didn't even want to talk with Shannon about what had just happened. I told her how much I cared for her as a friend, but that last night was just sex, and it was great but that was all it was for me. I could see just how much my words hurt her and just how rejected she felt was written all over her face. I couldn't think of anything except my own pain, couldn't get out of my own confusion to even say goodbye. She left my apartment and within a week was off to grad school.

Later that morning Lauren showed up. She just stood there at my doorway like she had not done anything to shatter me like she did. I could barely say the words, but I told her, "I'm having a really hard time with this."

"She frowned and countered with 'What, you don't think that I'm having a really hard time?'"

"Narcissist. Basically, saying that her feelings are hurt as much or more than yours are," Susan said, "Go on."

"She smiled and reached for me then almost pressed her way in the door, pulled me next to her, and said something like, 'Please hang in with me. I don't know why I left that voice mail except that he was increasingly suspicious. In just a few more months I can leave him. But right now, I really want to fuck you.' And so, we did."

"First of all, why was he suspicious if they were separated? Also, she doesn't sound like the romantic type to me. She seems mean and certainly pushy. I would have picked Shannon if I had been you."

I nodded in agreement, and this is where I suddenly felt sick with a wave of regret. Tears were right behind my eyes.

I told Susan that night was the first, last, and only day that I ever slept with two different women. I'm sure that some would find that exciting but to me it was only confusing and more than a little bit sad. Susan's first reaction was that making love with two attractive women in the same day might just be a lesbian pipe dream, but I explained that it was anything but that for me.

"It had only taken me a week or so to figure things out. But by the time I finally understood what I wanted, ended the relationship with Lauren, and gone to Princeton to see Shannon it was already too late. She had gotten together with Kim – another grad student. Kim moved into Shannon's apartment. They were newly in love, and they've been together ever since. I'm sure a lot of our friends think I must be a player because I've never had any relationship that lasted more than a few years, but I think I've always wanted to be in love and just haven't realized it. This is something so simple that millions of people do it every day, but it eludes me and always has. I thought I had it with Lauren, but I was a fool. I know I found it with Shannon, but the timing was all wrong. I don't even know what she will remember – we drank a lot of Tequila that night – but I hope that she will forgive me for the painful and selfish way I ended things that morning."

I will always remember what Susan said as she reached across the couch and hugged me, "Real friendship is a testament to forgiveness because that level of closeness requires bearing witness to our shadow as well as our light. Deep relationships depend on continued mutual forgiveness and mercy. Elizabeth, luv, not everything is going to be the way you think it ought to be, but this story might not be over yet. It is never too late if it is really love. Time will find a way."

Susan is a smart woman, and she is often right – but not always. I can only hope that this is one of the things she has told me that will turn out to be true.

Chapter Eleven: Shannon

I am tossing and turning and can't stop thinking about all the confusing emotions that are running through me right now. I am filled with overwhelming grief for Linda and missing her so much that I can't put it into words. As much as having everyone together helps all of us, her absence is even more noticeable as we reminisce about her. We are all feeling this strongly and that is obvious from the tears and the need we all have to hug and embrace each other. We are pulling together even more intensely than usual in our shared sorrow.

I am also so confused about Elizabeth. There is no question that I have always had a romantic and sexual attraction to her but that has always been concealed – just behind the veil of awareness – as Kim and I made our relationship work for all those years. But the way I'm feeling right now makes it apparent that this mantle has been lifted and something has ramped up since she arrived here earlier today.

It is so comfortable to settle into the warmth of these good friends and I recognize that this is what we all need to begin to heal. We've known each other for a long time and there is an easiness that comes with this familiar territory. Each one is a remarkable woman: strong, kind, smart, funny. I love and admire all of them and would do anything for them. Honestly, if anyone needed a kidney and mine fit, I would be first in line to give it. At our gatherings, we often use a quote from Rumi as a toast: "Friend our closeness is this: anywhere you put your foot, you feel me in the firmness underneath you." That is the depth and breadth of these friendship bonds between all of us.

In the last two months of Linda's life, I was with her almost every day. She had no energy to do anything but when she felt even remotely well enough Molly and I would crawl into her bed. She was always cold because of the chemo, so I would pile on blankets and snuggle next to her. Then we would be off on an hours long Netflix binge. Emily and I would make dozens of different kinds of smoothies with protein powder to give some nutrition since she had no appetite. Her mother and I helped bathe her when she was so sick and sweaty that she soaked through the sheets. Just before she lost consciousness this past week, I cut up an orange so I could touch her lips with the sweet juice, and she would smile. Each of these moments are emblazoned in my mind, and I am grieving for what she has gone through and admiring the courage she showed throughout her cancer journey. It broke my heart to see her failing, though it has been a privilege, an honor, to be able to accompany her in these final days.

This whole tragic experience has been a savage grace, the last gift of friendship from her that is genuine, intimate, and grounded in our affection for each other. She was my best friend and there was heartfelt closeness and tenderness between us just as there is with the rest of my Tribe. But what is not there – not for Linda or any of the others – is the intoxicating attraction that initiates a deeper, physical desire. A hunger so powerful, so present, that it consumes every moment of awareness. I realize that despite my love for each one of my good friends and their natural attractiveness, the only one that I feel this profound, passionate desire for is Elizabeth and this has always been the case.

I read an article about attraction in a psychology magazine and the author said that there are five main determinates of attraction: physical attractiveness, proximity, similarity, reciprocity, and familiarity. I have those in common with all the women in our Tribe. I cherish each of them and they are all beautiful human beings. But only Elizabeth activates an automatic, spontaneous – and definitely sexual – response from my body. Even when we accidentally touch my stomach flip-flops, I am as euphoric as if I am on an amphetamine high. When she is near me, my body warms up, and my heart rate increases so much and so immediately that I am afraid it could pound right out of my chest. I am turned on just by my fantasies about her. I have brought up her name in multiple conversations during the day even in contexts where this was not necessary and, perhaps, even a little bit weird. I can't get her out of my mind and I notice that throughout the day I have deliberately arranged my movements to stay physically close to her.

During my first year of high school, I had strong feelings for a classmate named Stephanie Foster. We were best friends. I didn't even realize that I was attracted to girls at that time, couldn't imagine this kind of crush, and it wasn't anywhere in my awareness to think that I could be gay. But what I did notice is that I took the long way around the hallways to get to my math class taking an unnecessary corridor because I knew that was the only time I could pass her, I would say 'Hi, Stephanie,' and she would smile and wave. I was written up several times for being late to class and I realized that I had plenty of time to get there except for this diversion but I was willing to risk it. I was fourteen.

That was more than fifty years ago but I'm doing the same thing right now to make sure that I'm sitting next to Elizabeth as our group moved from the patio bar, into the restaurant, and then to the pub for a nightcap. I am hoping this is not as obvious as I think it might be. I find myself watching her and I am constantly mindful of where she is in proximity to me. I'm trying to read these new signals that she is giving me. Are we really gazing at each other differently? Does her touch really feel so much more arousing today than it has for the last thirty years? I am hypersensitive to every cue, every response in my body with a singular focus to better understand what is happening here.

What powerful energy transforms strong ties of friendship into something infused with romantic passion? Eros the God of Love taking an interest? Cupid's arrow shooting down from the ether and landing with enough force to knock you off your feet? Limerence? Lust? Pheromones? Chemistry? Celtic warriors together in a past life? Some theories of reincarnation teach that souls congregate together.

It seems to me that Elizabeth puts out a magnetic field and I am helpless to resist it. An intense energy draws me in. She is like a planet that I have been orbiting for as long as I have known her. Up until today, that orbit has held steady and true but something in the field shifted, the orbit wobbles, and I am careening into her. I don't understand the basis for all of this. I don't know if these overwhelming feelings are the strong physical attraction or the emotional connection, maybe both. What I do know is that I am falling and falling hard.

In the Ballad of the Sad Café Carson McCullers wrote that the most outlandish people can be the stimulus for love and that – to the lover – the beloved might be treacherous, greasy-headed, and given to evil habits. The lover may see this as clearly as anyone else, but it makes no difference. The lover may shower even a mediocre person with a most wild and extravagant love. It is possible to fall in love with someone you may not even like but then not fall in love with someone you greatly admire and care about. But what happens when you like someone, and they are not treacherous, greasy headed, or given to evil habits? What happens when you already have a natural affinity for someone, a long-standing affection, are happy in their presence, and find this powerful desire to touch them – physically – in every way possible and to have them next to you? Then I imagine that could be attraction at warp speed. And I think that might be where I am right now.

My mind is spinning while contemplating this idea of attraction and the relationship between the lover and the beloved. But my cognitive freefall takes a sad turn as I think about what happens, over time, to that compelling energy that begins a romantic relationship. Where does it go when it vanishes? Does it simply disappear and dry up until it is nothing but dust and memory? Where did it go with Kim? Thirty years ago, we were madly in love, hot for each other. It was like a spark that could not be extinguished. So, what caused the shift from heart-racing excitement to boredom and profound disinterest? Is attraction only the stuff of beginnings? And then a year ago, it was gone, completely gone. Whatever Kim originally felt for me had vanished and been diverted to a new attraction. When she said she was leaving me it was like tumbling beneath a wave, unsure as to which way was up, and plunging deeper and deeper, unable to catch my breath. I have no idea why I was so unconscious that I did not see our love, our desire diminishing until one day it was gone and just as inexplicably and suddenly as it had first appeared.

I don't think that I can ever trust attraction again. I understand that there are no guarantees, no assurances, but I can't even imagine that I can ever have faith in a beloved who will not eventually break my heart.

Sunday

Chapter Twelve: Elizabeth

We are up just after dawn and don't see any lights on in the cottage where the Tribe is staying. Shannon is making coffee and setting out some yogurt and fresh fruit for breakfast. I've offered to help but she says she's got it, and I should just relax and enjoy this early part of the day since we've got a lot to do later.

"This is just a little snack to tide us over while those sleepy women get their act together. On Sundays, there is always a big brunch buffet at the restaurant, and I think we're doing it every day of this holiday weekend. I assure you that it will be overkill! There will be Bloody Marys, Mimosas, Champagne, a bunch of craft cocktails along with a coffee bar offering choices from all over the world. Of course, there will be a full Irish breakfast of bacon, sausages, baked beans, eggs, mushrooms, grilled tomatoes, potatoes and cabbage chopped into a hash called Bubble and squeak. And toast, marmalade, and lots of tea. You don't have to worry about Haggis, though. Megan drew the line saying it was more Scottish than Irish anyway and just too dreadful – and that is the word she used – to serve. She said she was certain that the kitchen crew would quit en masse if they had to start every Sunday morning dealing with Sheep's guts."

"Good God! UK friends tell me horror stories about Haggis. They call it Sheep's Pluck."

"More like Sheep's upchuck! So, while Megan has nixed sheep liver, lungs, and assorted innards she will have fresh fruit, melons, berries, oatmeal, whole grain cereals, and stuff to make veggie or fruit smoothies as a nod to healthy eating. But the main event will be eggs in all their glorious presentations including a create your own Omelet station, bacon, Taylor Pork Roll, sausage, hash browns, croissants, muffins, bagels and schmear, pastries, biscuits, pancakes, Belgium Waffles, French Toast, possibly crepes if sous chef Rachel is here today, and, don't forget grits for the southern girls…basically a celebration of everything that is filled with carbs or meaty. It's what Ryan calls the heart attack breakfast."

"Shannon, Stop! I just put on ten pounds while you are telling me all this. I might just have to stick with the Yogurt and berries you are serving up here!"

"Not a bad idea!"

Shannon is using the small aluminum coffeepot that sits on that gigantic stove. It is an old fashioned, non-electric percolator just like my grandmother had when I was a kid.

"Smells great, Shannon. Why do you use that coffeepot when you have this massive espresso machine right here?"

"I used to have that fancy Braun coffeemaker, you probably remember it, which was nice but entirely useless after Hurricane Sandy when there was no electricity for more than two weeks. I had this old coffeepot stored with some camping gear, used it, and realized that coffee brewed in a percolator is just better – like a lot better – and so it has the coffee job every morning. The espresso machine was a retirement gift from my colleagues and I think it requires advanced training as a barista to run it. I've never used it. I'll stick with what we've got, and you tell me if you don't agree that this is the best coffee you have ever had. Well, at least the best you will have this morning!"

I love the way she has redone this cottage, I can sit at the family table while she is in the kitchen and we can still see each other and talk.

There is a quiet knock on the door, and it's Tyler with my suitcase.

"Your luggage, madame," he says with a flourish. "I'll take it to your room."

"You are too sweet," I say. I follow him to the guest room, take a twenty dollar bill out of my wallet, and press it into his hand. "Thank you, Tyler." He nods, thanks me for the tip, and leaves.

"I'm almost sorry to see my luggage," I say to Shannon as I come back into the great room. "I was looking forward to trying on the rest of your wardrobe."

"No reason you still can't do that," she laughs.

This is just such an easy morning with two good friends who are so comfortable together that we can finish each other's sentences, and often do. I am checking my email on my tablet. Shannon's phone is on the table and the sound indicates that a text has arrived.

"Can you get that for me please? I'm sure it's one of the girls asking about what time we will be meeting for brunch."

I pick up the phone and see that it is not from one of the Tribe. "Shannon, it's from Kim."

She comes out of the kitchen, drying her hands on a towel. Her whole expression has changed as she takes her phone from me.

I heard about Linda and if you can handle it, I would like to come to the Celebration of her life on Tuesday. Just let me know. Kim

Shannon is quiet for several minutes and, once again, I see her stuff her feelings. "Everything okay?"

"Yeah. It is okay. This is the first communication I have had from her since the day we gave the keys to the realtor in Brooklyn. She walked down the street to Allison's car and the Lyft arrived to take me to the train station. It seemed like such a miserable way to end a thirty-year relationship."

Shannon tells me that Kim wants to come to the celebration of life for Linda. "Of course, she can come. She was friends with Linda for years and I would be some kind of asshole to deny her that. She asks if I can handle it. Well, I can."

"You've never talked to me and, as far as I can tell, you haven't told anyone – not even Megan – about what happened between you. I've tried to reach out to you – every one of us has – to see what we can do to help. When you told us that you and Kim were breaking up, we were all shocked, didn't see it coming. I am not pushing but if you want to talk, I'm always here to listen. Sometimes it helps to get things off your chest, Shannon."

She sits down at the table across from me and takes a deep breath. "I thought we were fine. We were like any couple together for all those years and we had lost a lot of the spark that brought us together, but we got along, never fought, and enjoyed a lot of the same things. I do not think we had a complete lesbian bed-death, but it was close. Over time, we both lost a lot of sexual interest in each other, but we still had affection. I just assumed that happens when a couple is together for a long time and life and responsibilities get in the way of passion. I don't think that only lesbians deal with this. My straight friends who are in long-term relationships tell me that this is almost expected. It was a Tuesday night just like any other. We were both home from work about six and I was making dinner. It was shortly after we saw you and Disney on Ice."

She gets a faraway look in her eyes and continues, "She said in serious voice 'we need to talk' a phrase which, in my opinion, always means wherever this is going will bad news. She told me that she loved me but wasn't in love with me anymore. Suddenly, I felt like all the blood drained out of my body and left me freezing cold. I could not catch my breath. Whatever your body does when it goes into shock is what I was feeling. I was shattered."

I move from my chair to the one next to her and place my hand on hers. She continues to tell me how Kim found "in love again" less than a month later with Allison, a mutual friend, and a frequent golfing partner of Shannon's.

"I was just getting to where I could almost accept what was happening and stop beating myself up for not seeing it sooner. After she told me she was leaving, I begged her to give us a chance. I pleaded with her to go with me to see a marriage counselor. How can you fix something when you don't know what is wrong? But she was resolute. We were finished. She didn't tell me about Allison right away but within weeks she admitted that she had fallen in love with someone else which, of course, I already knew in my bones. I insisted that she tell me who it was and she finally, reluctantly said that it was our friend Allison."

Shannon tells me that she was just getting to a place where she could understand and maybe even forgive. "I think we must be responsible for actions, but we can't always be responsible for feelings. Allison apparently gave her something that I couldn't. We had just run our course. You can have a good relationship but there's something that an 'old' one can never be and that's a 'new' one."

She goes on to say that Allison had been a casual friend to both of them and they all played golf and tennis and so there was a lot of interaction. I met Allison once when I happened to be in New York when Shannon and Kim had a party. She's attractive, a successful lawyer, and quite charming. But I cannot even imagine leaving someone like Shannon.

Their brownstone in Brooklyn sold quickly and when they were packing things and getting ready for the move Shannon came across credit card receipts that showed multiple occasions when Kim had charged for dinners, flowers, gifts on dates that made no sense.

"I found receipts for restaurants in Manhattan that she said were nights working late or she had to take a client to a business dinner, but I know she would have used her corporate credit card for that. There was evidence of a week-long trip they took together to Cape Cod at the time when Kim said she was at a CPA conference in Chicago. For the CFO of a Fortune 100 company, she did not cover her financial tracks very well. That is when I went ballistic. Elizabeth, when I put it all together it was obvious that they had been seeing each other for more than two years. And that's the part that I'm having trouble forgiving. She never even said she was sorry. What a fool I was."

"Shannon, do you think you are victim blaming? You are not foolish because you trusted what you were being told. Better to direct some of that anger to the one who was untrustworthy instead of the one who trusted."

"You're right and I know that intellectually. We should have talked more about what we needed but we became complacent as if the initial love that we felt would last forever without being nurtured or cherished."

She looks at me directly and I can sense and feel all the sadness that she holds inside. "I was within months of retiring from NYU, so I worked it out to teach most of the last semester remotely with only a few trips back to the city. We put the house on the market, and it sold quickly. I made the decision to move back to the shore. I am still writing my column for the Times and my blog which I can do from anywhere. It was good to be back here where I could help more with Linda and my Mom. I stayed in one of the empty cottages while this place was being renovated, tried to get engaged in some new projects with little luck, listened to Bonnie Raitt sing "I Can't Make You Love Me" thousands of times until I knew every word by heart. Since then, I'm trying hard to get out of this funk and this self-pity that is making me sick to be around me."

Shannon looks at her phone and texts a single line back to Kim.

I can handle it.

She stands up, takes both our cups, motions to me to ask if I want more coffee and says, "I'm not yet sure how this has changed me and whether I can ever really love like that again. Thirty years reduced to a cliché."

Chapter Thirteen: Shannon

As I promised Elizabeth, Megan and the restaurant crew put out quite a spread. We are lingering over coffee and discussing plans for the day. We have a little down time now, but the next two days will be wall-to-wall activity as we help the staff prepare for Linda's Celebration of Life.

It is a beautiful Chamber of Commerce Day with blue skies, a slight breeze, and temperature in the low seventies. Caroline, Nadine, and Barbara say they want to go for a walk while Tonya and Cindy elect to have a tour of the new kitchen with Megan. Marilyn lets us all know that she intends to continue to sip her Bloody Mary on the patio while reading the NY Times. As she finishes up the last of her breakfast, she smiles and says, "By the way, aren't waffles just pancakes with abs?"

"Goofball," Barbara says to her with obvious affection.

Elizabeth says she will be on the beach with the kids and their new kite.

"All those plans sound lovely," I say. "I need a couple of hours to finish my column for tomorrow."

"Oh no. I'm sorry you have to work," Cindy says.

"It is no problem. I have been writing this column in my head for more than a week. I've put my blog on hold until next Saturday. I should be ready to continue our day drinking by early afternoon."

Tonya asks me if I'm working on any other books right now.

"I have a half-done, and possibly half-baked, proposal to write about Queen Lili'uokalani who was the last monarch in Hawai'i. She was an amazing and interesting woman who most Americans – much less the rest of the world – know nothing about. If they realize anything at all about her it is that she was the composer of Aloha 'Oe and many other songs. But her music is the least of her legacy."

"Fascinating story. I have heard her name but didn't know anything about her, not even the song-writing part. When did she live?" Cindy says.

"She was born in 1838 and died in 1917. She was the last monarch of the Hawaiian kingdom. She was a progressive badass who led a resolute but peaceful resistance to US businessmen and other pro-American elements that wanted the annexation of the islands to the United States. They staged a coup d'état, and she was placed under house arrest and forced to abdicate the Hawaiian throne."

"What an interesting woman. When do you think you will finish your proposal?" Nadine asks.

I'm not even sure how to answer that. I've tried to work on it now for almost a year and I have made no progress. This is so unlike me. I wrote a 300-page book in less time and now we're talking about a twenty-page proposal for an editor who already enjoys working with me and is likely to be favorable to this idea for another project. But I keep putting this on the back burner. It is difficult to tell even these good friends just how exhausted I am and why I cannot concentrate. For the past year my mind and heart have been so tied up with Linda and with missing Kim that there hasn't been room for much else.

"It's hard to tell." Even though I have no real answer, it feels good to know just how much my friends support me in my work and in my life.

"All good things in their own time," Elizabeth says. "I'd say you've been quite busy with a lot over the past year."

I nod and I'm eager to get away from being the focus of this attention.

I am in my home office and almost finished with the column, at least the first draft of it. I go into the kitchen to get some ice water and from the window there I see Elizabeth on the beach with the kids. She is crouched down to their level and is explaining something to them. My guess is that it could be the aerodynamics of kite flying. She is smart about those kinds of things. Her documentaries are first-rate, have won multiple awards, and she has a unique ability to capture the essence and truth of complicated subjects but present them in a way that interested and intelligent lay people can understand. I once told her that she was like the late Carl Sagan who was brilliant, didn't dumb anything down, but explained complex astrophysics in a way that was comprehensible. "I'm pretty sure I'm not all that," she said.

I am so turned on to her that I'm not sure what to do next except watch her for a bit longer admiring her physical beauty and her ease of spending time with Jack and Patty. Their body language says everything: They are comfortable together, having fun, and, finally, they get that kite up in the air.

I finish the column or at least I have it to the most polished place that I can get it today and hit send on this email to my editor at the Times. I'm sure this is not the best column I've ever written but I've read it over half a dozen times, and it will have to do.

The front door opens, and Elizabeth and the kids come in. They are sweaty, salty, and sandy. But of course, they are!

"Have a seat, it looks like you could use a cold drink," I tell them.

They nod and I grab some glasses from the cabinet and a pitcher of iced tea from the refrigerator.

"Want some cookies, too?"

"Yes, please," Patty says as she looks at me. I nod and she goes straight to the pantry. She knows where the goodies are stored in my cottage and comes out with a package of Oreos.

"Aunt Shan, do you know that water does not look blue just because it reflects the color of the sky?" Jack says. "My friend Kevin told me that is why water in the ocean looks blue."

"Really?"

"But that is not the main reason that water looks blue. The reflection of blue from the sky is only a little part. So, Kevin is wrong. Water looks blue because of the way water molecules absorb light especially colors in the part of the light spectrum that are long wavelengths like red, orange, and yellow."

"It's like a filter," Patty says as she eats her cookie.

Jack is eager to tell more, and he looks straight at Elizabeth as he says, "And that filter leaves behind colors in the short wavelength blue band for us to see. Also, light bouncing off sediment and particles can sometimes make water look green."

Elizabeth smiles and nods. "You've nailed it, Jack!"

Jack smiles broadly at Elizabeth. It is so clear that he is pleased with himself as he takes another cookie from the package.

"Most of the ocean is dark," Patty says. "Light only goes down about 600 feet."

"And there is no light at all deeper than 3,200 feet," Jack adds.

"That's where the monsters live," Patty says.

"That part is not actually true, Patty," Jack corrects her.

"Uh uh, That's where they live, Dude," she says to him. He shakes his head and smiles at Elizabeth. We have all noticed that Patty is calling everyone "dude," these days. Especially but not only Jack. She's called Megan that multiple times and, once, I heard her talking privately to Molly calling her "dude."

I change the subject. "You guys really know a lot about water."

"Elizabeth told us about the color of water," Patty says.

"Elizabeth, I am impressed. Where did you get all this" I say and smile at her.

"When you make as many documentaries as my team has about rising sea levels, the disappearance of potable water in major parts of the world, and the future of the planet, you learn some stuff."

"Have a cookie, you win the day."

Patty reaches into the package of Oreo's and offers one to Elizabeth which she takes.

"Do you like cookies, Elizabeth?" she says.

"I do and these are awesome."

"Do you like Girl Scout cookies? Because I will be selling some in January."

"I will absolutely buy your Girl Scout cookies and those are the best, especially the Thin Mints. But no cookies that you can buy in a store or even from a Girl Scout are as good as the ones my grandmother used to make for my sister and me."

"What kind of cookies?" Patty is eager to talk about anything sweet.

"She made very old-fashioned cookies called Toll House Chocolate Chip cookies."

Elizabeth proceeds to tell the kids about the history of Toll House Chocolate Chip cookies and how in the late 1930's an Innkeeper named Ruth Wakefield in Wharton Massachusetts decided to add some broken pieces of Nestle semi-sweet chocolate to her cookie dough and expected them to melt into the rest of the ingredients. But they did not. They kept their shape, and the chocolate chip cookie was born.

I am always astounded by the weird facts that Elizabeth rattles off on any number of subjects. That is why she is highly recruited as a team member when we play Trivial Pursuit or other games requiring a bounty of what Linda called "perpetually remembered useless information." Nevertheless, Patty is impressed.

"They were, quite possibly, the best cookies in the entire world and she would put extra chips in them so in every single bite there is chocolate," Elizabeth continues.

"Will you make some for us? Please?" Patty asks with a pleading tone in her voice.

"Sure. I am happy to do that."

I am standing behind both kids and they can't see me, but Elizabeth can and I'm starting to laugh and shaking my head while giving her a glance that says, "Are you crazy and what the fuck! You have never made cookies in your life!"

She shoots a look back at me that says, "Please don't blow my cover."

The Third Act

And here we are on such an ordinary afternoon, eating cookies, drinking tea, and all I can think about is just how effortlessly she fits into my life.

Chapter Fourteen: Elizabeth

I have Molly on a leash, and we walk to the front of the hotel where Shannon will meet us in her car. We're going to visit her mother at Northview with a quick stop at the grocery store on the way. Shannon pulls up – I swear to God – in a car that is identical to the one she had in Richmond all those years ago: a 1973 MGB convertible.

"Shannon, this can't possibly be the same car that you drove in Richmond!"

"Not exactly, but a mirror twin, same model, same Cobalt Blue color, same everything though I did modernize a little."

The 1973 MGB is a British Sports Car that holds a driver and one passenger with a small parcel shelf behind the seats. This car is in pristine condition and the dashboard is, for the most part, classic except for a GPS screen showing a map. Shannon tells me that she also had Bluetooth and high-end Bose speakers installed to make hands free calls and run music from her cell phone.

"I sold my original car when we moved from Princeton to New York City. Honestly, owning a car in the city is a liability. There is never any place to park, and especially not in Brooklyn. I could easily get to work by water taxi to Manhattan and then the subway to my office. Starting the morning on a boat cruising the East River was, actually, a nice way to begin the day."

She opens the door, pats the parcel shelf, and Molly jumps in – she obviously knows the drill.

"We didn't need a car in the city. We'd take the train to the Shore and when we wanted to travel, we either went with friends or rented a car. We had a few great trips to New England with Caroline and Nadine. When I moved here, I knew I needed something to drive although Megan told me to save my money because the business owns numerous vehicles, sedans, vans, you name it. So, I always have transportation if I'm taking both kids somewhere but driving this car is less like getting to a destination and more like having fun. Maybe it's because it makes me feel young again or there is something about smoothly shifting gears with a manual transmission that seems like I am really driving. And then there is the understanding that the odds of this car being stolen are almost zero since most people under sixty wouldn't know how to drive it!"

"Are there still mechanics who tinker with or fix these old cars?"

"Yes! Our bartender Tony's cousin Paulie owns a garage that specializes in British sports cars. Once it was clear that I could get repairs as needed, the search through the Internet was on. I found just the right one and this is it. Paulie put in the upgrades, and he said they fit behind the dashboard like they were made for it."

Molly easily lifts her front leg allowing Shannon to put a harness on. Shannon clips that to a bolt on the floor of the shelf and explains this restraint. She says that Molly is a good passenger, but she is still a puppy. "I lock her in to keep her safe and because I have a fear that we will pass some guy on the streetcorner eating a hot dog and her she-wolf instincts will override all the training that we've done."

I laugh at the thought of that image.

I slide into the passenger side and attach my seatbelt. Shannon reaches over to the glove box and takes out a pair of goggles and her arm accidentally touches my knee as she pulls her hand back. Once again, I experience this now familiar rush of electricity when she touches me. I wonder if she is feeling anything like that right now.

She smiles at me and then puts the goggles on Molly who is sitting right behind us. "They're called Doggles and they protect her eyes."

As we pull out of the driveway, I notice a sign that I had never noticed before. It is round and white with the O'Connell Guest House logo and the words *Slan Abhaile.*

"What does that mean?"

"We just put that sign up this year. It's a Gaelic-language phrase meaning Safe Home and, in Ireland, that's what people say when you are leaving somewhere and heading home. Get home safely. Be safe. Almost like a blessing for a safe and smooth journey, traveling mercies. It's a lovely thought, really. Though during "the troubles" in Northern Ireland the Irish Republican Army plastered it on murals as a farewell to the British Armed Forces. I once saw a photo showing that some daring vandals spray painted this phrase on a British tank which seemed less like a prayer and more like a go home, mofos!"

She makes the right turn, and we are moving now. It's a warm day and we are in a ragtop with Fleetwood Mac blasting through the speakers. I am reminded of all those times thirty years ago that we drove around Richmond in a car just like this one heading to parties, retreats, concerts, and other gatherings of our Tribe. This was long time ago to be sure but, at this moment, I know that if I ever want to feel young again, I'll ride in a classic British Roadster driving alongside the ocean on a sunny day with a good friend, rock and roll blaring, and a dog wearing goggles sitting behind me.

We stop briefly at an Acme grocery store to pick up some of the ingredients I'll need to make the homemade Toll House cookies that I promised the kids.

Shannon turns off the engine and pulls on the parking brake, looks at me, and with a serious expression or, perhaps more like a faux-serious expression says, "You know, Elizabeth, I'm not trying to be critical, and you have so many excellent skills that I can't even count them all, but cooking, baking, actually doing anything in a kitchen is not exactly your long suit."

We both start laughing because my reputation as the worst cook among all of us has been well-known – and well-deserved – for all these years.

"Refrigerated slice-and-bake cookies are not that bad," she offers.

"Not what I promised, those would be referred to as 'semi-homemade,' Shannon. That is not the same thing."

"Okay, Ina Garten. Please give me your list and I'll get what you need. This is where I shop, and I can do this fast. I know where to find everything."

She takes the recipe I printed earlier today.

"Please do not forget to get an extra bag of chocolate chips. You know so the cookies will be just like my grandmother used to make."

"Oh, right!" She smiles, walks to the entrance of the store, and I can't take my eyes off her. I relax in the seat, enjoying the warm sun on my face, and take in all the comfort I feel when I am near Shannon. How easy it is to be with her. At this moment, I allow myself to release some of the sadness – if only for a moment – about Linda's death that has enveloped me for weeks. I pet Molly and say, "What are we going to do with all this, Molly Girl?" She doesn't answer but her big brown eyes convey lots of affection and I suspect that what she wants more than anything is for Shannon to be happy.

The Northview Progressive Care and Rehabilitation facility is a fifteen-minute drive from the grocery store and is on the mainland, so we take the bridge off the island and into Stafford Township. Northview is an attractive combination of four-story brick buildings designed in a horseshow shape surrounding a courtyard that is a green space with neatly trimmed grass, flowering trees, and dozens of Knock-Out Roses. Old fashioned streetlamps line paved walkways and a scattering of small benches combine to make this landscape look inviting. I can see past the building and this complex is on the shore of Manahawkin Bay and except for the brick sign noting the name of this place, it looks like an upscale apartment or condo community.

Shannon has told me that elderly people and those with disabilities that need residential care can start here in an active adult community then, as needed, move to various degrees of assisted living, and, finally, to several stages of skilled nursing care. In the past week, the staff has told the O'Connell family that Anna will be moved to a new level in the memory unit. She is getting worse, more confused, less functional and none of that is a surprise because that is the course of this cruel illness. I once read a book about the journey of families who have loved ones with Alzheimer's Disease. It was titled The Long Goodbye and there could not have been a more apt description. My grandmother died from this disease when I was in my fifties. She lived twelve years from the day she stopped recognizing any of us until the day she passed away. I wept when she died but my greatest grief was on the day, years earlier, when she looked at me and had no idea who I was. I understand what Shannon and her family are going through right now.

Shannon puts a leash on Molly and the three of us walk to the front door. The woman at the reception desk greets Shannon warmly and comes out from behind the desk to pet Molly.

"Jackie, this is my good friend Elizabeth."

"Nice to meet you, Elizabeth. We're always happy to see Shannon and, especially Molly. She is our best therapist."

Molly laps up the attention and wags her tail as Shannon removes the leash.

At the end of the main hallway is the Day Room which is large and sunny with wall-to-wall windows that look out over the Bay for a million-dollar view. There are about thirty people here in various states of wakefulness. Four women sit at a square table, talking softly and playing cards. There is a middle-aged man in a wheelchair reading a magazine and these people are the high end. Everyone else appears to be much older and they are all sitting quietly in chairs, some dozing and some staring into space. There is easy-listening music playing in the background but except for that the room is quiet. All that changes and the energy feels more charged when Molly enters. The shift is palpable, and it is no wonder Jackie said that Molly was their best therapist. Some who are almost asleep in their chairs, reach out their hands, making clicking noises with their fingers and calling quietly to her though no one uses her name. Molly begins to make the rounds and work the room.

I see Anna immediately. She is sitting in a wheelchair next to the windows facing the Bay. I have not been with her in more than two years, but she looks ten years older than I remember. She is still a beautiful woman with the same hazel eyes that her daughters share but hers are clouded in a way that theirs are not.

Shannon pulls up a chair next to her mother, kisses her on the cheek, and takes her hand.

"Hi Mom. Hey, Elizabeth is here to see you, too," as she points to me. I pull up a chair and place it on Anna's other side.

Anna looks at me and smiles, but it is obvious that she has no idea who I am. What is more heartbreaking is that she has no idea who Shannon is either and I am filled with sadness for both of them. Molly comes right to Anna's side, wagging her tail and whining. Anna pets her and makes little kissing sounds with her lips. My hand is resting on the arm of her chair, and she places her hand on mine. I put my other hand on top of hers give it a soft squeeze and bring it to my lips and kiss it gently which makes her smile again. We are holding hands and I can feel that she is almost skin and bones, but her hand is soft and has the fragrant scent of Jergen's Lotion that I recognize as the same moisturizer that my grandmother favored.

Shannon and I continue to chat with her mother as if she knows what we are saying. Shannon tells her about the kids and things that are happening at the Guest House. She doesn't mention Linda's death though I know that her Mom was close to Linda. I talk about the kite I brought the kids from London and a documentary that is in the works and will be shot in Ireland. I don't think Anna is taking in a single thing that either of us are saying but she pays rapt attention anyway. We are like this for the better part of an hour when one of the nursing staff approaches carrying a small box.

"Shannon, we have a few things of your mother's that we're giving to you for safekeeping. There is not a good place to keep them in the step-up section of Memory Care,"

Shannon thanks her and takes the box. "Mom, we'll be back in a couple of days. Ryan and Judy will be here tomorrow to spend some time."

Shannon kisses her mom on the cheek, I move my chair back to its original location, squeeze Anna's shoulder and we walk toward the door. Shannon puts the leash on Molly's harness, and I offer to carry the box.

The box is small and not heavy at all, I can see a copy of Shannon's book in there, rosary beads, and a small photo album. The framed photograph on the top shows Anna and Michael on their wedding day. They are young and smiling.

Their whole life ahead of them. Michael has written a message on this photo to his new bride: *To my Anam Cara – now and Forever Love, Michael.*

"Your parents are so beautiful and so young."

"Yes. Babies. On the day they were married Mom was twenty-two and Dad twenty-five."

"What does that mean? Anam Cara?"

"It's two Irish words. Anam means 'soul' and Cara means 'friend.' So Anam Cara literally means Soul Friend. It refers to a relationship that is so close, so intimate that there is no separation. No space between them."

"Like a soul mate?"

"Yes, but more like a soul mate on steroids. There is no good translation into English because the Irish language is so much more poetic and profound. The Celtic imagination believed that souls radiate around the physical body – like an aura – and when two souls connect on a deeply spiritual level, their souls mingle, and they become one. It is about an endless, eternal relationship that goes beyond the material world into the realm of spirit and the sacred. Enormously powerful and romantic idea. I think it is almost like what Plato wrote in *Symposium* about humans originally being two selves in one. Then somehow, they get separated and so we spend our lives looking for our other half. When you find him or her there is an ancient recognition. It is like you remember that person from a time before you even knew you were you. Aristotle, other Greek philosophers, and Greek mythology called it *two friends, one soul.* And when these two recognize each other and fall in love, they come home to each other. It was always meant to be, but it is love that opens the door."

"I think that I might have slept through most of my philosophy classes, but it sounds like what Mary Oliver wrote in her poem *Oxygen*: *"It is your life, which is so close to my own that I would not know where to drop the knife of separation."*

Shannon smiles at me. We have known, and for a long time, that Mary Oliver is a favorite for both of us. "You may have slept through Introduction to Western Philosophy, but you clearly did not during your studies of the best American poets of this century."

Shannon opens the boot and I place the box in there. "I'm glad I had a chance to see your mother with you, Shannon. I know this is hard."

She smiles at me and nods. She remembers that I had this same experience with my grandmother years ago and she was always supportive, including a visit to her while fielding the rudeness of the rest of my family who showed little respect for either of us.

"Thank you for coming here with me today, Elizabeth. You understand more than anyone what it is like to watch someone you love disappear before your eyes."

She looks like she is about to say something else but instead motions to Molly to get in the car and she hops back on the parcel shelf. Shannon hooks her in, and we are ready to go.

"You know it is so difficult to accept that no matter how hard you work or what you accumulate – even in a well-lived life – in the end we are all reduced to just a small number of things. To me that really brings home – what matters is only what we hold in our heart and in our memories and the love we leave behind. I'm sorry that your mom and family must go through this, but I do think she knows just how much she is loved. And she seemed comfortable and happy to see you."

"I hope you are right, Elizabeth. Megan and I talked about how we could best care for mom and about eight months ago it was clear that she needed more help than we could provide. We had a family meeting, kids included, and decided that residential care would be best for her. But we could only accept it if at least one of us would see her every day. We have done that. We keep a schedule but its flexible and so far, we've made it work for everyone."

Once again, I am close enough to see Shannon pull back tears, but I still don't know how she does it.

"A month ago, one of Megan's friends was curious about why one of us comes here every day since mom doesn't even know who we are. Megan knew the question was asked kindly and with real interest and just said, because we still know who she is."

"And that's what matters."

Even through the sadness behind her eyes, Shannon looks at me with such affection that I want to throw my arms around her and comfort her. I think that in the past and as her good friend, I would have done exactly that, but we are skirting this new and unexplored energy between us so, instead, I just reach over and touch her hand.

We are more subdued on the ride home and instead of Fleetwood Mac we are listening to Joni Mitchell's Blue album, and it is well suited to how we are both feeling now.

Then she turns to me, smiles and says, "One of the best parts of the day still lies in front of us."

"What's that?"

"Seeing you make these cookies from scratch!"

Chapter Fifteen: Shannon

Elizabeth sets out each of her carefully measured ingredients in separate small bowls, positions the recipe she had printed, puts on her glasses, and gets ready. I insist that she wear my bib-apron since she is dressed in navy blue and almost all her ingredients except the chocolate chips are white and powdery – this could be an unfortunate combination. She is setting up as if she is a surgeon beginning a major operation. And I am wondering if she is making cookies or conducting a science experiment.

I've seen Elizabeth working in the kitchen before – as we all have – and she is really a mess. She is such a terrible cook, and she knows it. And thank God she has a good and self-deprecating sense of humor about it. She claims that when it is her turn to make dinner, she makes reservations. Now she can prepare excellent and imaginative salads but even that wasn't there at the beginning like when she once asked if she should sauté lettuce. I thought that Tonya's eyes would roll into the back of her head. Salads represent the sum of her culinary expertise so it remains to be seen how these cookies will turn out.

One of the memories that we continue to remind her of happened on July Fourth weekend twelve years ago. We were all here at the shore to celebrate the holiday and planned a cookout. Elizabeth found a recipe for Strawberry Cool Whip pie and insisted on making it.

"Any recipe that requires Cool Whip as the main ingredient has to be hideous," Tonya said as she sipped her wine.

"Nevertheless," Elizabeth countered as she showed Tonya the picture in the magazine where she found this recipe. "It will be light and refreshing."

Elizabeth was alone in the kitchen, and it was a separate room in those days. She declined any help so the rest of us were at the table playing Cards Against Humanity – a game that had just come out. Linda was especially good at it since it involves answering questions with outrageous, funny, and often lewd answers. All I remember is that we laughed until we were sick.

"Where's Elizabeth?" Barbara asked as she came in the door after walking their new puppy. They named him Duffy – an adorable twelve-week-old Boston Terrier.

"She's in the kitchen," Cindy answered.

"Unsupervised!" Marilyn said.

"Oh, look out!" Linda said as she scooped up her winning cards.

I noticed that Duffy was constantly in and out of the kitchen.

"Can Duffy have a strawberry?" Elizabeth called out.

"Yes, but only a few. They're high in fiber and Vitamin C and good for dogs in moderation but they have too much sugar for him to eat a bunch," Barbara answered.

Somebody made some crack about Barbara and Veterinary school, but I can't remember who said it. My guess would be Marilyn.

Things were relatively quiet in the kitchen for thirty minutes and then we heard a loud crash and Elizabeth yelled, "Ohhhhhh, Fuuuuuuuuck!"

We all raced into the kitchen. She was flat out on the floor covered with red Jell-O Cool Whip mess everywhere. She was holding a bowl almost empty now but with the rest of that pie filling in it. Most of it was on the floor around her and slopped over her face, hair, and clothes. I knelt by her head to see if she had cracked it open and if I could tell the difference between blood and this red sticky Jell-O mixture.

"Don't move her until we know nothing is broken," Kim said as she sat down next to her. Linda went to her other side.

"Are you okay, Elizabeth?" Kim asked.

"I'm fine. Nothing is broken. I slipped, that's all."

Linda took Elizabeth by the hands and helped her to sit up. "What happened?"

"I had never made Jell-O before, and the box said I could use the 'speed-set method.' Put ice in it instead of just cold water to make it set up faster. I thought it was taking too long, so I did this. It was almost to the right consistency, so I reached into the bowl to retrieve what was left of the ice cubes, but when I pulled my hand out it was coated with a thin layer – a patina really – of Jell-O. Almost like a surgical glove. And that made it hard to hold on to the bowl."

Someone, I'm not sure who let out a muffled laugh. Again, my guess is Marilyn though at this point we all realize that Elizabeth is not hurt and deliberately used a whacked word like 'patina' to describe what just went on here.

"Okay, it gets worse," she said. "I used a bowl that was not large enough and I didn't get a good grip on it because of the Jell-O hand and when I was trying to take it to the refrigerator per the recipe just the movement of getting there caused waves of oscillation and it started to overflow the sides."

"Waves of what the fuck?" Marilyn said.

"Is that when you fell?" asked Caroline.

"Not exactly. No. That comes next. Earlier I had given Duffy a strawberry and I thought he had eaten it, but he didn't finish it. He only chewed it up and left it on the floor. As I'm headed towards the refrigerator, the heel of my shoe landed on that half-chewed strawberry and now you know the rest of it."

The kitchen is covered with a red splattered mess, and it looks like a murder has taken place in here. This image is only made worse by the fact that Elizabeth had played tennis before this pie-making nightmare and was still dressed in tennis whites – or what used to be white.

Linda shook her head at Elizabeth, laughed and pulled her toward her and tightly embraced her. "You are a disaster, girl!" Now the two of them were covered in this slop and we sent them both to the outdoor shower but before they got out the door, Tonya took a fingerful of the Jell-O Cool Whip from Elizabeth's shoulder and tasted it. "Mmm. Not as bad as I expected it would be. Actually, it's quite tasty!"

As they are going out the front door, Marilyn exclaims, "No one is hurt. So then let the mocking begin!"

"Excuse me, Shannon, are you laughing at me or what?"

"Not laughing at you but I was just thinking about that Cool Whip fiasco."

"Oh, for God's sake. I'll never live that down."

"True."

"Okay. Back to the present moment, time traveler. I need to preheat the oven to 350 degrees. Can you help me?"

I must admit to her that I've never used the oven before and, in fact, when I open the door to it the Owner's Manual and paperwork from the purchase are still in there.

"You've never used your oven?"

"No. I've made coffee and heated up soup on the burners but nothing in the oven.

I bought it because I thought that I would get back into cooking again but then between all the time I was spending with Linda and my overall sadness about Kim, I just never used it."

"Well, then I am delighted to be the charter member of your cooking club to use this big honking expensive as shit oven."

When you meet Elizabeth, you will be struck by her physical beauty, her obvious intelligence, and her quick wit. But you have to know her well and spend time with her to appreciate that she can also be very cute and even a little bit ditzy. Like right now. She has pushed her glasses up on her nose and left a trail of flour on her cheek. I go over to her and wipe that off with my thumb and we have touched in this kind of way for thirty years but this time I feel that energy – this intimacy – that has been occurring between us since she arrived. I want to take her in my arms and kiss her but instead I move to the stove and start setting the pre-heat for 350 degrees and change the subject.

"Hey," I say, "Did you know that they released an album of the Joni Jam from the Newport Folk Festival with Joni Mitchell and Brandi Carlile?"

"You're kidding. What an amazing performance that was. Joni Mitchell is such an astonishing woman. Anyone who can come back from a near-fatal aneurysm, relearn everything and then perform for thousands of people has my undying respect and not to even mention the catalogue of songs she has written. I've been a fangirl since the Laurel Canyon days but now I think she might be my spirit animal. Would you download it for me from iTunes?"

She is up to her elbows in cookie mix. .   laugh

and tell that I'm happy to do that for her.

I pick up her phone from the counter,

password."

"Elizabeth Matthews no spaces," she says. "Skippy0t

"I know that 0613 is your birthday in June. Who or what

"Skippy was my grandmother's dog."

I laugh. "Elizabeth, the two things the experts tell you never to do when constructing a password is to use your birthday or the name of a pet. And here you are with both in your Apple password. This makes it easy for hackers."

"Have you ever been hacked?" she asks me.

"Yes, twice."

"Me? Never. Not one time even with my substandard password."

We both laugh. We need this respite from sadness, from all the feelings about Linda and the visit to my mother in the nursing home. I realize that throughout all the years of our friendship that she, more than anyone, has always been able to bring me to a better and happier place whether consciously and deliberately or just by being with her. I can't help myself and despite the charged energy between us right now, I put my arms around her waist and hug her from behind. "I'm lucky to have a friend like you, Elizabeth."

116

Monday

Chapter Sixteen: Elizabeth

We are sitting at a big table on the patio bar and although it is barely noon, we are still sipping the Bloody Marys and Mimosas from today's brunch. We have been talking about the relationship between free will and destiny and I'm not quite sure how we got here again from a discussion about celebrity women who are in their sixties and seventies and beyond and are still hot. Marilyn insists that Cher is two hundred years old. "I swear she was an adult and singing with Sonny when I was a tiny child." But Nadine is saying the same thing about the connection between destiny and free will as the British astrologer had told me years ago: There is simply nothing about moving forward in life that is separate from free will and that is why clear prediction is impossible – from every practice of divination – to foretell the future. Because you don't know in advance how someone is going to act or the choices they will make.

"It is an interesting question," Nadine says. "The Tarot has some unique ways of looking at this dynamic. It is not destiny versus free well as much as it is destiny AND free will. They are bound by a delicate and intimate relationship. Like a dance between lovers."

Caroline urges Nadine to show us and Nadine says she'll go get her deck of Tarot cards.

While we are waiting for Nadine to come back Shannon suggests that we go inside because it is going to rain.

"The Weather Channel said bright and sunny all day," Cindy says.

Shannon points out to Cindy the beginning of a front that is moving rather quickly toward the shore. "The Weather Channel doesn't always get it right." Shannon smiles and I have a hard time taking my eyes off her. When she is relaxed and with friends her whole face lights up, her smile is bewitching. On this morning, she takes my breath away.

As we pick up our drinks to move inside, the wait staff takes that as a cue and begins to bus our table.

There is a large corner dining booth with several chairs near the fireplace in Sean's Pub – they call it the "family table" and we stake our claim there. By the time we are settled Nadine arrives with her Tarot cards.

She says she wants to be clear that there is nothing in destiny that does not include free will and is hammering this point home. She explains that she is using the Rider-Waite deck and, even though there are many versions of these cards, this is the deck that she learned on.

"Who will volunteer," she asks.

"I will," Phillip raises his hand like we're in a classroom. "Pick me!"

Nadine smiles and explains that there are any number of ways to throw the cards, many different spreads that provide a variety of information. Some of the popular ones, she says, are The Celtic Cross, The Spiritual Guidance Spread, The Five Card Cross and there are many more. The Tarot deck consists of seventy-eight cards divided into two groups: the major arcana, which has twenty-two cards, also known as trumps, and the minor arcana, which has fifty-six cards. Either because there are so many cards and several people raised their hands for a reading when Nadine asked who was interested or because we have all been day drinking since brunch, Nadine suggests a very simple reading: A one-card pull using only the Major Arcana.

Phillip moves from his seat up next to Nadine and she instructs him to first ask a question.

"Like what?" Phillip asks.

"Questions such as: What should I be grateful for? What does my future look like? What do I need to know about the immediate days ahead? How can I be a better friend or partner? What am I being asked to pay attention to today? You can ask any question really, but it must be about yourself and clear, specific, and heartfelt."

Nadine zips through the deck of cards and pulls out the twenty-two that are the Major Arcana. She puts the others aside and shuffles the ones in her hands just like any deck. She then fans them out face down in front of Phillip. "Now just let your hand hover over the cards and pull the one that you are most drawn to."

Phillip moves his hand back and forth over the cards and finally picks one.

The card is The Empress. "Oh, darlin' that is so perfectly me. Even better than a Queen!" he says in the campiest voice he can muster. He gets a laugh and especially from Rafael.

"What does that mean?" he asks Nadine.

She explains that The Empress is associated with Venus and the element of Earth. Pulling this card relates to fertility, abundance, creativity. "This is a powerful card because it may represent a new idea, business, or project in your life. Did your question relate to any of those? You can share the question you asked if you would like but you don't have to."

"Well, this is interesting to me. I asked if I would get the job of choreographing a new show. I know the director quite well and she indicated that I am in the running, and they should decide by next week. It is a musical adaptation of the Stonewall Riots and I want it so badly. You might not think there is ageism on Broadway because everyone is creative and open-minded. But, girls, you would be wrong."

"The Empress card portends a positive outcome," Nadine smiles.

"You will let us know when you get the job? Caroline asks.

Phillip nods and motions to Tony at the bar for another drink.

"Who's next?" Nadine asks as she looks around at the group.

"Shannon needs to go. Come on, Shannon, you're the hostess with the mostest of this crowd," Marilyn says.

Shannon holds her hand in a stop sign. "I think there are lots of people who want to go first."

The group starts chanting "Shannon, Shannon, Shannon."

"What is this Middle School peer pressure for the AARP crowd?" she laughs. "Okay, okay."

Phillip moves from the chair next to Nadine, curtsies to Shannon and she takes his place.

Nadine puts Phillip's card back into the deck and shuffles them again to clear the energy although Phillip pulled an optimistic one and if I were Shannon, I might want to share some of that.

"Okay, Shannon. Same instructions. Think of a specific question and then pick the card that calls out to you."

Nadine fans the cards in front of Shannon and she picks one.

She pulls the Death card and takes in a breath. I'm thinking that of twenty-two cards that this one might be the most unnerving given that we are gathered here because of Linda's death.

The Death card in the Major Arana is a scary image and shows the grim reaper dressed like a knight clasping a sickle and riding a pale white horse. On the ground are dead or dying people from all classes: kings, bishops, commoners. In the corner is a bright yellow setting or rising sun.

"Oh shit. That can't be good."

"*Au contraire,*" Nadine says.

"In some decks this card is called 'the card with no name' or 'Death/Rebirth.' It is about change, Shannon. It is about death but not physical death. It signifies letting go of things that no longer serve you or the end of a major phase or aspect of your life. It is the opening to possibility for something more valuable and essential. This card is renewal and transformation. It's a good omen, Shannon."

"I think you've just been psychoanalyzed by a card, Shannon," says Marilyn in a sweet teasing way.

Tonya moves into the seat next to Nadine and Shannon sits down next to me.

The rain has gone from a drizzle to a full-fledged downpour. As the storm increases, the crowd at the bar does the same. People are coming off the beach and from the pool and the patio bar. The mood is jovial, everyone entering now is soaking wet and half of them are in bathing suits as they raced for the shelter of the pub.

Shannon sees the crowd piling up to the bar. She goes over and talks briefly to Tony. She comes back to the table and whispers to me that she is going to help before he gets overwhelmed.

"I'll go with you," I offer.

She smiles. "Yeah, that would be great."

Shannon nods to Tony and we walk to a door I had never noticed that is just to the left of the bar. She puts in a code, opens it, and we go down a short flight of steps to the wine cellar. It is much dimmer and significantly cooler than where we were.

This wine cellar contains hundreds, maybe a thousand bottles. The interior ceiling and floors are a rich, polished Walnut as are all the racks for bottles. Shannon shows me that there are two doors into this area: one from the pub and one from the restaurant. She says that temperature, humidity, and level of light are all critical to storing wine. An iPad type tablet is attached to the wall near the dumbwaiter, and she explains that this is the inventory system, so they know immediately what they have, what they need, and trends about sales.

"The temperature here is always kept at approximately fifty-five degrees, humidity at sixty percent, with low light levels. Bottles are always stored either horizontally or at a forty-five-degree angle with the cork facing downward so that it stays moist, and no air gets into the bottle."

"Who knew wine was so exacting, so temperamental, such a diva," I say.

"Right?"

Even though wines of all types do well under these conditions, she tells me that O'Connell's keeps the whites in a part of the cellar that is a few degrees cooler since they will be served colder than the reds. In addition to the wines there is a section for Liquor and a Beer Cooler with cases of beer along with dozens of kegs.

"We have really improved our game since we hired Maria. We never had a sommelier before and when my parents first started, this was a snack bar serving hot dogs and two types of canned beer: Pabst Blue Ribbon and Budweiser. Now we have twenty craft beers on tap. And there is a huge difference between what we sell in the Pub versus the restaurant. The restaurant is heavy on wines and craft cocktails. The pub? Beer, Irish Whiskey, beer, beer, and more beer. Three of our taps are devoted entirely to Guinness."

She walks over to an intercom button, pushes it, and says, "Tony, we've got the Chardonnay and a bottle of Ketel One on the lift. Do you need anything else right now?"

"Oh, and two bottles of the Outback Shiraz and a fifth of Jameson," he says. We can hear the laughter and noise of a crowd behind him. Shannon walks to another area for the Shiraz, grabs a bottle of Jameson, puts them on the lift and then goes back to the intercom. "Last call. I'm coming back up," she says. Tony says that's all for now.

She is putting these items into the inventory computer, and I am not sure what comes over me. I don't know if it is the dark, cool environment, our proximity, the flirting that has been going on for the past two days, or the thirty years I've waited to feel her body next to mine. Since I've been here there have been small, seemingly accidental touches, lingering eye contact, fueling the intense attraction that I have. We know each other on so many levels but I am uncertain. If I have misread the situation, I might jeopardize our long-standing friendship. Over all these years, I've been careful not to intrude on boundaries as good friends. I am tentative as if I've never kissed a woman before when, in fact, I have kissed this woman. But that was a long time ago. I am standing directly behind her, and I softly call her name. She turns to me and. I put my arms around her and kiss her. I feel her body respond to my touch but I'm still not sure what to expect.

She looks directly at me with that same lingering eye contact that made me make this bold move in the first place. This is the way we have been looking at each other since that initial hug in her cottage two days ago.

"Are you going to seduce me?"

"Yes."

"Good," she whispers as she puts her hands on my face and pulls me closer. She kisses me with a tenderness that astounds me, and I take her in with all my senses. Her lips are soft, her hair fresh with subtle notes of jasmine and citrus. I put my hands on her waist and pull her toward me. She moves easily. My mouth descends from her lips to her neck, and she throws her head back giving me access. I am stirred, and I want to take her right here, right now – immediately lost in the passion of holding and kissing her. My whole body is throbbing with an ache, a desire that has waited so long for this moment. Her hands are on my hips as she pulls me closer and moves against me in a slow rhythm. She slides her hands from my waist touching every inch of me as she kisses me deeply. Her hands are in my hair now and her kiss has a new urgency. Our excitement is intense. Breathless. Hearts pounding. Our bodies were designed to be joined together like this. This is a dance of anticipation, and I want to envelop her in my every cell.

"Earth to Shannon! Earth to Shannon! Are you okay down there? Is this fucking intercom working? We're in the weeds up here and can use your help."

We are stunned out of our embrace and the heat that has just exploded between us.

I am still holding her as she leans over to push the intercom button. We are both gasping.

Shannon pushes the button. "We'll be right up, Tony."

"Good. Because it is truly a MAYDAY situation!"

I pull her close again, kiss her passionately and she responds. I can feel just how turned on she is. Her heart is pounding as is mine. She whispers in my ear, "Is spontaneous combustion really a thing?"

"God, I hope not." I say softly as I kiss her one last time.

Chapter Seventeen: Shannon

Emerging into the pub from the wine cellar feels like a bucket of cold water poured over my head. The air is twenty degrees warmer, the light ten times brighter, the noise of many people laughing and talking deafening. If those were the only sensations, I wouldn't feel so rattled. I know that my face is flushed. I touch my lips and I can still feel Elizabeth's on mine. I'm sure that my hair is wild. I run my hands over my blouse. Note to self: Don't wear linen if you are going to make out in the wine cellar.

The saving grace is that this place is jammed, and I don't think anyone notices that I'm weak in the knees and confused. This is Labor Day weekend at a popular resort and the rain is driving everyone off the beach and out of the pools. Our friends are still at their table but have been joined by some others looking for an empty seat. I just heard Tom blow the air horn telling all guests to seek shelter because the storm has upped the ante and now includes thunder and dangerous lightning. They are three deep at the bar, every chair and table is full, and this place is as jammed as it gets thirty minutes before closing on Saint Patrick's Day. In addition to our guests, the pub is popular among locals and visitors who are not staying at the Guest House. They all seem to be here today.

Ryan is behind the bar with Tony and signals to Elizabeth and me. "You are deputized." He smiles and hands each of us a bar apron with an order pad and a waiter's corkscrew in the pocket.

"Just bus tables where you can, take some orders and bring them to Tony or me. Maria is on her way to help. We really fucked up. It was supposed to be a bright, sunny, dry day and we staffed accordingly, expecting late afternoon to be swamped and mid-day to be soft with everyone on the beach. Some of the staff are on their way in but could be an hour or more since most of them were out doing whatever they do when they aren't expected until late in the day. No one will be here immediately so it's just us to the rescue. We're the calvary." Ryan smiles. He never seems rattled no matter what is going on.

Elizabeth ties the apron around her waist and grins at me. She takes the waiter's corkscrew out of the pocket. It is loud in here and she leans in next to my ear, "I have an electric corkscrew and one of those wing things. I have no idea how to use this," she says to me. She starts to move away then she turns, looks at me with that lingering gaze, leans into me, and whispers, "I really want you."

Having her this close to me and feeling her breath on my ear after what just happened is stimulating to say the least and not helping me to calm down at all. She goes to a table of young guys who have met the most minimum requirement of 'no shirt, no shoes, no service.' I can't hear her, but she is making friendly conversation, and these guys are laughing and are most likely flirting with her. The light blue cotton shirt she is wearing emphasizes her beautiful eyes and I have been lost in these eyes for the past two days. Elizabeth gives me a thumbs up as she delivers four draft beers to that table. An easy order. Wait until they start asking either of us to recommend wines or craft cocktails. Honestly, we are the B Team of wait staff.

I am bussing tables and taking checks to the register when I see Elizabeth struggling with that waiter's corkscrew. I go over to help but Cindy and Tonya beat me to it. They have owned a successful restaurant for twenty years and Tonya is showing Elizabeth the finer points of this device. It is a tender moment of friendship, and I am moved by how close we all are and how remarkable it is that we have this after all these years.

The rest of our crowd clears their table making room for some of the folks coming in from the rain. Every one of them is now helping to bus and wait tables and run drinks to customers. Tonya and Cindy are behind the bar slinging beers with Ryan and Tony.

Phillip comes up and whispers to me, "This is a lezzipalooza of wait staff!"

I smile at him. He and Rafael are such a wonderful addition to our group. They have been nominated as "Honorary Lesbians" with tee-shirts to prove it which they love wearing at the pool.

The last time the whole Tribe was together in this room was three years ago. I had, surprisingly, won a National Book Award for Nonfiction and didn't even know that my publisher had entered it. I was happy that a book about women who accomplished so much for this country but were forgotten by what is commonly taught as American History won this award. Years ago, when I decided to write it, some of my colleagues told me I wouldn't be able to find enough compelling stories to fill a book. They were so wrong.

Megan and Kim cooked up an author signing at O'Connell's to promote the book and celebrate with me. On that chilly November afternoon, the staff decorated the pub with balloons and streamers, Congratulation signs were slathered over almost every available bit of wall space.

Megan and Judy were greeting people as they entered and selling my book as they came in the front door. Kim sat beside me at the signing table opening each book to the proper page to sign which I had just learned is best on the title page rather than the first page. My publisher told me that makes the book more valuable if, in fact, I ever became a famous author.

The place was packed with locals and friends from the community. Linda and her entire family were there, each with a book to be signed. I know that

Megan and Judy were doing a super sales job because I had already given Linda a signed copy when it was first published.

My Mother was next in line with a copy of the book. "Mom, you already have a copy of this book. Did Megan and Judy put the big 'buy one get one free' pitch on you?"

Mom smiled. "We are all so proud of you, Shannon." She leaned across the table and kissed my cheek.

I signed the book to her:

To Mom…the most important woman in _my_ history and with all my love, Shannon

Ryan was next and had both kids and each of them held a book to be signed.

I pointed to Patty, "She can't even read?!"

"Yes, I can!" Patty lied.

I looked up and the next person in line was Elizabeth. I was shocked to see her. She had two copies of my book.

This group can certainly keep a secret. I had no idea that Elizabeth would fly in from London for this little event that I later learned was merely the opening act for a great surprise party. I jumped up from behind the desk and embraced her. She was smiling and laughing. The rest of the Tribe was behind her in line: Caroline, Nadine, Cindy, Tonya, Marilyn, Barbara. All buying books though I had already sent each a signed copy.

"Oh my God!" And then there was a flurry of hugs and hellos, and I couldn't believe that no one gave away a single thing about this gathering.

I am lost in memories of how these women that I love have always come together and am reminded of a story attributed to anthropologist Margaret

Mead. A student asked her what she thought was the first sign of civilization. People were expecting an answer such as finding a fragment of pottery, proof of planting crops, or art on a cave wall. Dr. Mead said that it was none of those things. Instead, it was evidence supplied by a 15,000-year-old skeleton found on an archeological dig. This individual clearly had a thigh bone that had been broken and then had healed. A break here will take at least six weeks to mend and until it does walking is impossible. If you broke this bone 15,000 years ago, you would certainly die. No one could survive this break for that long and they would have been eaten by predators before they were up and moving on their own. This healed bone demonstrates that someone had taken time to help this fallen person, had bound up the wound, carried them to safety, and fed them. Someone helped a fellow human rather than abandoning them and it is those indicators, said Dr. Mead, that show us when civilization began.

I think back to that early human who was saved by others who cared, who carried her or helped her to limp along, brought her food, and tended to her wounds. She must have been surrounded by a loving tribe just as I am and so, I'm inclined to agree with Margaret Mead about evidence of the first glimpse of civilization. I am always touched by the support and loyalty of these women, our tribe, this chosen family. These are my friends who are attached to my heart and for almost half my life. We have been there for each other in good times and bad. We've seen each other through the seasons of our lives, and we are still here – together – after all these years. I am so lucky to have this container, this sense of belonging because this is not a luxury in life. For all people, throughout every culture and every time, the deep human need to belong is essential. It is like air.

Chapter Eighteen: Elizabeth

The rain stopped as suddenly as it had started. And at about four o'clock people begin to leave the pub and go for a last dip in the ocean or to finish their beer by the pool. We all find our respective seats back at the big table.

"God, working in a restaurant or a bar is a hard work," Caroline says.

Tonya and Cindy share a sly glance and then Tonya says, "You think?"

More than anyone, except perhaps Marilyn, Tonya has a sharp and a somewhat sarcastic wit. She and Cindy have created an extremely popular restaurant in Carytown – the most bohemian section of Richmond – and have taken it from a small café to a Southern Cooking/Caribbean fusion foodie destination that draws customers from all over central Virginia and beyond.

Caroline laughs. "I get it!"

I can hardly take my eyes off Shannon as she quietly says, "How did we all get so lucky to find each other?"

"Luck or destiny?" Nadine asks.

"I don't really know," Shannon answers. "Maybe that intimate dance you talked about, you know, destiny and free will. I would never have been in Richmond except that William and Mary gave me a full scholarship. My family wanted me to go to University of Pennsylvania or Rutgers, but I think that was mostly my mom who wanted to keep me close."

"I would never have landed in Richmond until the Army threw me out,"

Tonya says.

"What?" Nadine asks. She doesn't know this part of our history.

When she graduated from high school, Tonya – who is strikingly beautiful – had two opportunities: work for a premier modeling agency in New York City or accept a nomination to West Point. "Modeling clothes and makeup? Are you kidding me?" She said and before she could explore any other options, she was off to upstate New York for a commitment to "Duty, Honor, Country." This was the initial class that admitted women and Tonya was the very first African American woman to receive an appointment.

"It was 1983, I was stationed in Germany, and it was a full ten years before Clinton's Don't Ask Don't Tell policy. Gay men and lesbians had no place in the military, even those who had attended one of the academies. I made the mistake of going to a gay bar in Amsterdam while I was on leave. Someone outed me and that was the end of my military career. My choices? I could resign voluntarily with an Honorable Discharge or fight it and be court-martialed."

Tonya explains that she went to Richmond because she had previously been stationed there and still had a couple of friends in the area. "It's hard to find a new career when your whole professional life has been as an Army Captain." She went to Babes bar, applied for a management position, got it, and stayed there for the next twenty years.

"And if I had been well paid to coach basketball I never would have looked around for some bartending shifts," Cindy added as she reaches over and touches Tonya's hand.

"And if I didn't play softball, I would never have met any of you," Barbara added. "God, Cindy, do you remember all the team names you tried to get the league to accept?"

"What was wrong with Killer Dykes or Sappho's Sisters or the Amazon Strikers?" Cindy asks innocently.

"I think they were trying to get away from the perception that all women who play softball are lesbians," Barbara says.

"Well?"

"Not all softball players in those days were lesbians," Cindy says. "There were a bunch of straight women who played."

"Really?' Marilyn asks.

"Just kidding!" Cindy says.

We laugh and remember how hard it was to get into so many leagues. The team's name problem was solved when Tonya and the owners of the bar agreed to be the sponsor so now it was just known as 'Babes' and no one could argue with that.

"And if I had not been a klutz and broken my ankle during tryouts, I would never have managed your team," I add. "Because I wanted to get on another team and then they didn't want me after that. I guess a player on crutches doesn't make for a winning season. Babes was the dumpster of those teams where everyone else was cut-throat and beyond competitive. You just said, 'Can't play? Well then you can manage us!"

That was such a long time ago, but every memory is clear as if it happened yesterday and that softball culture was one of the few places that lesbians at that time could safely congregate, make friends, and maybe if they were lucky, find someone special and fall in love.

"You don't seem so klutzy these days, Elizabeth," Shannon says. I smile and nod.

"That remains to be seen."

"Do you remember a songwriter named Dory Previn?" Caroline asks.

No one knows who she is talking about, but Nadine says with a smile, "I'm sure we are about to find out!"

Caroline tells us about Dory Previn – a songwriter and poet in the 1960's who had won several academy awards for music and lyrics she had produced for films. She was married to a world-famous symphony conductor Andre Previn, and she went crazy when he left her for a much younger Mia Farrow.

"Who can blame her for that?" Nadine adds.

"How do you remember all this shit?" Marilyn says. "I thought Elizabeth was the only one who clogged up her cerebral hard drive with all this stuff."

Caroline continues unabated, "Anyway she wrote a song called Children of Coincidence and it is about how tiny decisions or little bits of chance affect big trajectories in our lives. Something about 'if I hadn't made a left-hand turn if you hadn't made the right.' I can't remember all the words though."

"But Dr. Google can," Barbara says as she punches in the information on her phone and then reads what she finds."

If I hadn't made a left-hand turn

If you hadn't made a right

If I'd waited just a moment more

If you'd missed the light

If that car had never blown its horn

If that friend had stopped to talk

We'd have never met at all

If I didn't take that walk

I'd have gotten there too early

You'd have gotten there too late

We are children of coincidence

Coincidence and fate.

Phillip says, "Fascinating! We would never have heard of this place, if Shannon's friend Colleen didn't have the flu and gave her matinee tickets to her. She and Kim came. I went looking for Colleen – I had not listened to her voice mail saying that she was ill and gave her seats to good friends. I met Shannon and Kim and fell in love. Well, in a platonic manner of speaking, of course. We became friends. Shannon invited Rafael and me to an event here more than twenty years ago and we have been tight ever since."

I realize that these chains of destiny or luck depend not only on choices that we make but they are linked to choices that others make as well. If my father had not taken that job in Richmond, I would have attended high school in Chicago where we had lived since, I was born.

"Linda lived here within a mile of our summer house, and I never even knew of her until I met her in Richmond at Babes, and we started talking. Do you remember that one time after the softball tournament?" Shannon says.

"Yes. You had that blind date with that mean woman who was the one who asked you out and then wanted you to pay for the whole date, I'll bet. At least that was always her reputation," Cindy says.

135

Shannon smiles and nods. I remember meeting her that night and even though I was already involved with Lauren I felt an immediate attraction, thought she was beautiful, funny, and just exuded a kindness or goodwill that was hard to explain. I was glad to later learn that this blind date didn't seem to be going anywhere but didn't understand my feelings at the time. Not at all. I don't add any of this to the conversation.

"And if my friend hadn't brought me chocolates from her trip to Europe and if Linda didn't love chocolate and if she had not offered to clean my room for a month for just one little piece of it, and if we didn't laugh, eat chocolate, and become fast friends I would never have met any of you. I was closeted at the time even though the Art Department was probably the most liberal one on campus. But Linda kind of zinged onto me with her gaydar – which she always claimed was as near to perfect as anyone can be – and invited me to that softball tournament…" Caroline fades off as our thoughts return to Linda.

"Call it luck or destiny. Whatever it is or has been is more important than I have words to say," Tonya says.

"We are tethers for each other," Marilyn adds. "We keep each other sheltered and, as we are seeing that right now, we will need that more and more as we go forward in our lives."

"Tethers. Do you remember that NASA photograph of an astronaut who stepped out of the Space shuttle Challenger and had the first untethered spacewalk? He had nothing but a small jet backpack or something that would allow him to maneuver back to safety. Otherwise, it was just him – one fragile human being against the black vastness of space," Shannon says.

"That was American astronaut Bruce McCandless in 1984," I add. That picture is entirely clear in my mind, and it is still one of the most famous photographs ever taken in space.

"Thank you, human Google," Marilyn says to me with a laugh.

"Do you all remember Linda telling us that photograph was one of the most frightening images she had ever seen," I ask.

We all remember. How could any of us forget it? Linda made it so clear that this terrified her.

"It scares me about what life would be like if we didn't have this Tribe to help us through right now and what we will experience in the future," Cindy says.

And I am thinking about so many things. Would this attraction and the feelings that I have for Shannon push through these coincidences had they gone another way? What if my father had never taken that job in Richmond? What if Shannon had gone to Rutgers instead of to a university near Richmond, Virginia? Does the pull of that destiny where it is 'two friends, one soul' or the route to one's Anam Cara have the capacity to overwhelm the everyday decisions that each of us make that change our destiny irrevocably and forever?

I could spend the rest of my life pondering these ideas but, right now, all I can think about is how it felt to kiss her, and I am looking at her right now as if there is a real possibility that – maybe this time – the stars have aligned, our destinies have intertwined, and we might get this right.

Chapter Nineteen: Shannon

We have been summoned, as Ryan has called it, by Megan to come into the restaurant for a special dinner with wine pairings that she has arranged. No one can be more annoying than a bossy older sister. And no one can be as endearing as this sweet woman who has always taken care of my friends and me. It is like she is generations older – not just two years – when she takes charge like this.

She has reserved the best location in the house for us. This is one where we can see the ocean and is far from the activity of the bar and the swinging doors to the kitchen. There are seats for all of us and she has set a place for Linda at the head of the table. The silverware and glassware are there, the chair is leaned up against the table, and there is a single red rose in a bud vase in the center of the placemat. I watch the moment that Elizabeth sees this, and her eyes tear up immediately. She is just like Megan, I think. How I envy them this immediacy of emotion that they both seem to have and that is so foreign to me. I must work to process what I am feeling and I'm not always good at it.

Megan is directing the seating, and she is deliberately putting Elizabeth right next to me. I smile at her, and she raises an eyebrow but I'm not quite sure what she means by that.

We are all seated, and the wait staff has served our drinks. I love this restaurant. Even if it were not my family's, I would appreciate the quiet ambience, the view of the ocean, and the competent and totally responsive staff that is a result of careful hiring and even more exacting training. The investment in the restaurant has been huge but it is paying off. We get great reviews and that is a result of meticulous planning and my mother's philosophy. She said, "Put the right people in the right spots and give them what they need to do their best." She was a high school English teacher, my father was the business management guy, but she had a natural affinity for having a vision and making it work. That was her philosophy about taking the plunge to make this investment. So far it is working.

Megan comes back to the table and introduces us to the two main players in the success of The Lighthouse Bistro.

I am waiting for her to speak when I see Elizabeth looking at me and I gaze back at her and smile. I think it must be obvious beyond words about how she has affected me and is doing so even right now.

"I would like to introduce you to our Dynamic Duo. Our Executive Chef is Aiyana Bergeron. She is from Ontario with more than twenty-five years of experience in some of the best restaurants in New York City, Boston, Montreal, and Detroit and studied at the Culinary Institute of America.

Aiyana is a not-quite fifty-year-old woman with striking dark brown hair and eyes. I tell Elizabeth that her background is almost like a fairy tale. Her father was a bush pilot from Detroit, met and married her mother who is a Chief in the First Nations Cree tribe living in and around Ontario. She is creative, inventive, and loves the idea of pulling together cultural food traditions.

Megan introduces Maria Hernandez, our sommelier. She is in her early forties, from Colombia and is a second degree – a certified sommelier – out of four possible and there are only about three hundred of those in the world. Marie is one of six from South America and the only woman. Still, she studies for the next level that is called advanced.

"The requirements to become a sommelier are crazy. They must blind taste and identify wine and be able to tell where it came from, including whether it is from the north bank of the river or the south. How far from lavender fields in Provence were these grapes grown?" I lean into Elizabeth. I don't know if I am whispering so that I can move closer to her or because I don't want to interrupt Megan's flow. Either way and in a move that is completely unlike me, I quietly put my hand on her knee, and she looks at me. We both know what is happening here.

Aiyana and Maria begin to describe the meal they are about to serve.

Aiyana welcomes us and reminds us that there are other options including a Beef Bourguignon and a Vegetarian choice as well as anything else from the menu. But the course they are recommending tonight is Horseradish Encrusted Pan-Seared Sea Bass over garlic mashers, over wilted spinach.

"Sea Bass is a firm, mild fish that has an inviting texture. This is a wide species of fish. In the southern part of the United States, a favorite in many coastal locales is the larger fish called Grouper. But you do not have to be a major seafood lover to enjoy this presentation and the horseradish gives the fish a notable and fantastic finish. We'll begin with a fresh salad combining seasonal vegetables, strawberries, goat cheese, and pine nuts with a light and tangy vinaigrette. We'll finish with a house made crème brûlée, coffee, and dessert wines. And now, Maria will give you more details on the pairings."

Maria is barely forty years old but has been studying the science of wine since she was twenty-two and newly graduated from university. She begins to tell us about our wines for tonight.

Elizabeth leans toward me and whispers in my ear, "Now that I know that wines are, in fact, divas, we are about to learn that there is more to them than whites and reds."

And she is right, of course, but mostly I wish that she had more to say. Feeling her this close excites me and I'm not sure how much more I can hold after the kiss in the wine cellar and this extreme physical attraction to her.

Maria continues with her recommendations: "For our fresh salad course, we have a Sauvignon Blanc from Stags Leap winery in Napa Valley, California USA. Of course, champagne and prosecco are perfect for all the pairings that we will talk about tonight."

Maria suggests the Richioli Estate Chardonnay from the Russian River Valley in Sonoma, California for the Sea Bass, and Sauternes, a classic white sweet wine from Bordeaux, France for the dessert.

When Maria finishes, these two young women stand together with their hands behind their backs like troops who are now relaxed and at ease. They smile at each other, and it is apparent that they like and respect each other. There is an easy affection. They must know that they are better together than apart and understand why Megan says they are the "dynamic duo."

Megan pulls up a chair just between Elizabeth and me. "What do you think?" she says.

Elizabeth tells her that these women are unbelievable and no wonder this restaurant is soaring like it is. Megan motions to Maria who comes by to say hello.

Megan is bragging about her and Aiyanna. She looks a little embarrassed but hangs in there. This is her boss, after all.

Megan tells us about how creative these two women are together and that have made even the off-season work in terms of business.

"Most people here think we are only a three-month business – between Memorial Day and Labor Day - with a couple of weeks of shoulder season but that was before there were reasons to come out for a delicious meal and enjoy being with friends," Megan says.

"Ariyana and I put our heads together to think about ways to bring people to the restaurant during the cold and dark early months. In the summer, we are packed and must turn down reservations. This is not the same in February, March, or even any time after Christmas," Maria tells us.

All of us were concerned about how this new restaurant would work in the dead of winter. Like many coastal resort communities, the population changes on any given day from more than 200,000 in the season to less than 10,000 year-round residents.

Megan tells us about how they have arranged off-season events like tastings from various areas of the world pairing food and wines and, often, with a content expert speaking about that country, its customs, foods, and people. We have had others with unusual approaches such as 'Screw this!' where only wines with screw tops are considered. No corks allowed. And what I think might be my favorite: Wine pairings with Girl Scout Cookies. We have had to offer three times the tastings to fit in even most of the people who want to come to these. Patty is a new Girl Scout, and the restaurant donates a portion of the profits to Girl Scout programs and her troop. The Scouts sell cookies from January through April and that's the time that there are no tourists in town, and we could be in the doldrums until at least the beginning of May.

"What are some of those pairings," Elizabeth wants to know she is so curious about this one.

Maria smiles and asks, "Which cookies?"

"Thin mints," Elizabeth answers.

"By far the most popular of all the Girl Scout cookies. I would suggest any full-bodied red like a Cab or Syrah. Personally, I like Goosecross Game Farm Cabernet Sauvignon from California," she answers immediately.

"Last year, Ryan told us that he had only eaten one Thin Mint. We later learned that by 'one' he meant one sleeve of them," Megan laughs.

"Okay, how about Tagalongs – kind of peanut buttery." Elizabeth asks.

I can see that she is into this now.

"Yes. Peanut butter and chocolate – like the most exquisite combination of flavors imaginable. That is an easy one," Maria says, "A juicy red wine like a Zinfandel or Malbec. Almost any Tawny Port works well here with a taste that is like sipping on a PB&J sandwich. I like Mascota Vineyards Unanime from Argentina."

"One more. Samoas?"

"There is no beating this combination of coconut, caramel, and chocolate with a definite and satisfying crunch. I'm always partial to a peachy Sauternes dessert wine. But any Rosé with berry, melon, or citrus notes would pair well. For an interesting and somewhat indulgent taste yet less conventional pairing pull in a full-bodied Malbec. Maybe Tank Garage Winery Wild Child Rosé. If you can get it, 2021 was one of their best years."

Once again, I put my hand on Elizabeth's knee under the table. I am trying to be mindful about why we are all here, but I am even more captivated by her with each passing moment. And I am not sure how much longer I can contain these strong feelings. Watching her interest in the wine pairings with Girl Scout cookies just reinforces to me just how alive she is and how curious she is about almost everything. I have no doubt that, in the future, she will find ways of helping us all to know just what wine to have with our Girl Scout cookies. She doesn't forget things like that. I love to watch how she engages with the world and just how much I want to touch her.

Chapter Twenty: Elizabeth

It has been eight hours since we kissed in the wine cellar, and I can barely contain myself throughout the extraordinary dinner that Megan arranged. I push my food around my plate hoping that no one will notice that I'm not eating. I have no appetite. The staff presents a different wine paired for each course, but I toy with them and only sip a few. I know where this is going, and I want to be absolutely sober. Everyone is talking, laughing at old stories, crying about Linda, and toasting to her life. I stay in each of the conversations as best I can. But I am completely distracted and most of what we are talking about is hazy because all I can think about is that kiss and now, sitting next to Shannon and feeling the warmth of her thigh next to mine. We continued that deep, lusting eye contact throughout the afternoon which did not make anything easier. Twice she touched my knee under the table, and I thought I would lose it.

I am still not sure why we are being so secretive about what is going on between us. We are both single now and our friends would certainly be happy for us if we were to reveal these feelings. I'm sure that some of them – probably all of them – can sense something in the vibe we are putting out for each other. Still, the timing doesn't seem right to let the Tribe in on what is going on. We're here for Linda and still have the Celebration of Life to complete. And Shannon and I have still not talked about that night thirty years ago and how it went so wrong. We are in uncharted waters if we are transforming from good friends to lovers. I don't even know what this will mean, and I don't think she does either. I do know we need to manage this energy carefully so that we do not injure the enduring and close friendship that we have. But at this moment being careful is the last thing on my mind.

The sun is casting long shadows across the compound and starts to set as the blue sky over Barnegat Bay blossoms into pink and then into a blazing orange. It is a gorgeous sunset, and a few want to sit on the beach and watch the last light of day give way to the full moon rising over the ocean. But we all agree that it will be a busy day tomorrow preparing for Linda's Celebration of Life and so most of us head to our cottage for an early night. More than four hundred people are expected tomorrow and there is a lot we need to do to help Megan and the staff. We say goodnight to our friends. They head to their cottage as we go into Shannon's. We barely make it.

We are reaching for each other, and literally stumble in the front door though neither of us has had more than a glass of wine. We are in the same room where two days ago we embraced as long-time and close friends grieving for Linda. An affectionate hello, a hug, a recognition that held a promise. I knew in an instant that there was something different in the energy of that touch. Something had heated up between us that is both powerful and palpable. Whatever passion we felt for each other thirty years ago that had been sublimated, transformed into a deep and abiding friendship was no longer able to be hidden or pushed aside. Those constraints fell away when Kim left her and neither of us are compelled any longer to honor a relationship that is over or to hold back this attraction. Though until the moment of that embrace, I was not fully conscious of just how intensely I had longed for her. And now, at this instant and with a sudden awareness that leaves me breathless, I realize that everything I have ever wanted is right here.

Tonight, we hold each other tightly with the full length of our bodies intimately touching and I cannot keep my hands off her or my lips away from hers. That initial embrace that held such promise is being realized as we reach for each other, and our passion is being fully expressed.

At this moment, I am not certain we will make it into the bedroom or if I will take her right here. She pulls me closer and kisses me deeply, mouth open, her tongue touching my lips. We struggle to get to her bedroom and, once there, I carefully guide her to the bed. I want to direct what is about to happen.

I lower her onto the bed and straddle her being careful to keep my weight on my knees. We are making constant eye contact as I pull my shirt over my head, unfasten my bra, and toss them both on the floor. I sense the change in her breathing, and she reaches for my breasts and cups each one. A shiver of electricity burns through my body and the throbbing between my legs reaches a fever pitch. She attempts to sit up, but I gently push her back while I begin to unbutton her shirt. Truthfully, I want to rip that shirt off and have her now but, more than that, I want to feel everything about her completely, slowly, present for every movement, every moment, every memory. I want her all night. I slide my hand under her shirt and feel her breast. She takes a long breath. Our eye contact telegraphs the deep passion we are feeling and doesn't stop until I kiss her. Then her eyes close and she moves underneath me as I slowly continue to unbutton her shirt. She reaches her hand to help me, but I place it on the side of my face while I kiss her fingertips. I will do this.

I am on top of her, remove her shirt, and as I lean forward to kiss her our breasts touch and I am no longer certain that I can go slow. I shift to her side while firmly placing my thigh between her legs. She takes a sharp breath. While I am holding her like this, kissing her, I slide my hand down to her waist, unbutton, and unzip her shorts. My hand slides under her briefs. She is so wet for me. I pull both off and I remove my shorts and the length of our naked bodies are skin to skin and I am overwhelmed with desire and the softness of her. I feel every inch of her, every one of her heartbeats against me. I take her face in my hands and kiss her deeply.

I have had more than a few lovers over the years. Each time, I was seeking something more than sex. I yearned for feelings that not only touched my body, but my heart, my soul, in some profound way. I have had some lovers who stayed for a short time, a few months to a few years. I hungered for something that felt enough like love to see me through until the real thing appeared. With one other woman, besides Shannon, I thought I had found love only to discover that it was false gold and a terrible heartbreak in my life. But, in all my sexual experiences, I have never felt like this before. Because what I am feeling right now is fundamentally different. I am amazed by the total abandon of any constraints, the rapture of being fully alive and immersed in her. I am finally home. I am known, understood, and cherished and she is showing me that in every beautifully real way.

Our bodies have both changed over time but, at this moment, to me, she is just as beautiful as she was thirty years ago. What has not changed is just how she responds to even my slightest touch. What has not changed is the gentle curve of her lips, her softness, and how she moves from tender to urgent in a single breath. I remember every detail from all those years ago. I remember it all.

Slowly, I move my lips from her mouth and kiss her neck and shoulders. Her hair is splayed across the pillow as I touch her. I can't take my eyes off her. I kiss her again and again as my hand cups her breast. I move my lips there, delicately scraping my teeth against her, until I slowly encircle her with my tongue as her nipple hardens under my touch. My other hand pulls her closer to me as she whispers my name, her breath on my ear pushes me into an even greater arousal. At this moment, my hunger for her has no bounds.

She presses closer to me as my knee takes command of her center. Her breathing increases as I slide my fingers between her legs, between her lips and softly touch her there. Her hips rise to meet my hand more firmly as my thumb finds its mark and she gasps as I rotate it in slow circles. Her arms reach out for me, and she has her hands in my hair. While my thumb is stroking her, my fingers enter her and firmly move in unison. She spreads her legs wide for me and moans as I pick up speed, thrusting resolutely while my other arm holds her tightly pressed against me. She is giving herself to me with a power and a passion that increases my desire and nearly knocks me out as an orgasm overtakes her. Every muscle in her body is on fire and reaches a crescendo as she moans, trembles, releases, and then slumps in my arms. I am close to a climax myself, but I am still inside her and by the thrumming of her body I know that she has more to give me. I kiss her as I whisper her name and continue to fill her with my fingers, and she goes up again against my touch and surrenders. She climaxes again and again until she is still, and I slowly slide my fingers away and collapse on top of her.

I lie against her back, kissing her neck and shoulders as I pull the quilt over us and settle in with my arm around her and embracing her breast. Without a word, she touches my hand and entwines her fingers in mine. In all the thrilling ways in which I have just experienced her body, it is this simple, intimate touch that makes my heart explode.

Tuesday 5:15 am – The Day of Linda's Celebration of Life

Chapter Twenty-One: Shannon

I feel Elizabeth leave the bed the second her hand slips away from me. I had the deepest, most restful sleep I have had in more than a year and just thinking about last night arouses me.

Her touch is powerful because it is, at once, tender but absolutely determined. Every intention, every behavior, every sensual gaze expresses that she knows what she wants, and she is going to have it. No one ever before her – not even with Kim when things were good – has ever been able to coax every bit of passion from me with such immediacy. We have only made love once before last night and that was a lifetime ago, but Elizabeth seems to have confidence that she intimately understands my body, knows what thrills me, and is generous in giving everything to me. She is engaged and anticipates what I need from her at every moment. And it is this effortless loop of connection and communication with our bodies that makes this moment transcendent, spiritual. I am fully aware that this is not just sex but something much more than that although I am hesitant to name it.

The anticipation over the last two days and leading up to last night is striking to me. Ever since the first embrace when she arrived and everything since then – every flirtatious touch, every minute of eye contact, every time her voice softens as she says my name – has compelled me to a peak of arousal. It is possible that foreplay started at the moment of that first touch. I don't even know if it is healthy or normal to be constantly turned on for days at a time, but I do know that this is how I have been since she arrived.

And when she kissed me in the wine cellar, I literally thought I might implode. I know about kisses and how the passionate kind releases dopamine and oxytocin that stimulate the same area of the brain that responds to cocaine and heroin. And then and just like with drugs, euphoria and addiction follows. And that is exactly how I feel. I am filled with a joy that has eluded me for more than a year now and longer than that if I am being honest with myself. And then I realize that I am immediately addicted to her. I want more of her – everything – and I want it now. I don't know how I got through the dinner and the hours longing to touch her, to kiss her again. And I feel guilty about that – of course being Irish I am already somewhat prone to guilt. All our friends are here, we are grieving for Linda and all I can think about is her hands on my body and kissing her, touching her until she peaks, and then goes limp in my arms. Megan must know something is up between us because she was insistent about seating Elizabeth next to me. Twice during dinner, I touched her knee under the table. I didn't have a choice or so it seemed. I just knew that I had to feel her body under my hand and that I couldn't wait even one more minute.

She is in the shower, and I have fantasized about making love in this shower since it was installed. The imaginary lover at first was Kim – at least the Kim I remember before she broke my heart. Then the fantasy changed to a made-up woman, a fictional lover who does not and never will exist. Despite my imagination, it never occurred to me that a real-life passionate encounter would be with my good friend who I have loved in a different way for most of my adult life. If my desires are even remotely accurate, it will be amazing. If I don't drown.

I walk into the bathroom, open the shower door, and step in. She smiles at me, "Good Morning." I smile but don't say a word. I'm not here to talk.

My intent should be clear because there is nothing ambiguous in my movements. I do not break contact gazing into her eyes as I position myself in front of her and reach for the body wash. Quite deliberately – slowly and methodically – I rub my hands together turning the soap into fragrant suds and then I start with her neck. She takes in a breath, closes her eyes, as my fingertips tease down her shoulders, over her breasts, stomach, and the curve of her hips. I slow down as I trace her inner thighs and linger between her legs. Her breathing is sharp and fast as I softly stroke between her lips, and she shudders under my hand. She was not expecting this yet. She is wet and moving her hips closer to my fingers as she sets her hand against the shower wall to steady herself.

Carefully, I turn her so that we are both under the showerhead washing away the soap. I lean into her and kiss her passionately, my tongue tasting her lips as water cascades over us. Slowly, I start my way down her body – kissing her neck and shoulders. I savor each movement as I trace the scar on her left breast with my fingertips. This is the most beautiful thing I have ever seen. An emblem. A signature that she is here today. Alive and well. I track that same line with my lips kissing her over and over there. She moans as I put my lips against her nipple and take her into my mouth, it is already hard as my left hand strokes her other breast. My tongue caresses her as she takes a ragged breath. Her arms surround me as her fingers dig into me.

Taking each moment to fully engage her body, I kiss my way down until I am kneeling on the shower floor. There I focus my attention between her legs and tenderly spread her open. She takes an intense breath as my tongue finds the source of her pleasure and slowly at first, I stroke her there. I have my hands on her hips to balance her and to maintain the right pressure. She moves her hips towards me and her body tenses. Her hands are on my shoulders, squeezing me hard. The taste of her on my tongue and lips is exhilarating and I am out of my mind for this woman. At this moment, I have only one aim, only one desire…to give everything I have to her.

I continue stroking her with my tongue, take my fingers and enter her thrusting gently but firmly and now my body is on fire. My speed increases and I feel her throbbing against my flesh.

I can't get enough of this woman. I want to touch her everywhere with my fingers and lips. My fingertips are sensitive to her every response and feeling everything. Every receptor in my body is on high alert to this passion between us and the ways her body replies to my touch.

The Irish word Acushla is used – between lovers – as the word 'darling.' But the deeper meaning is 'pulse.' And that is what I want right now, I want to feel every part of her. I want every beat of her pulse, every fiber of her being, every inch of her body, every vibration of every cell. I want all of it and she is giving it to me.

Her hands are on my shoulders squeezing me hard as I rise off my knees and pull her toward me holding her close while my fingers continue their relentless advance. There is a precise moment – before it takes place – when you know that you are going to climax. You have hoped for it, most likely even expected it. But it is only in that blaze of rising passion that your whole body realizes that you have reached a point of no return. What is about to happen is inevitable and you could not stop it if you tried. You no longer have any choice, and it takes you like a riptide.

I sense the instant when Elizabeth's body reaches this pinnacle as she moves her hips further into my hand. Her heart races and she is gasping, every muscle is shaking. She trembles and moans and then surrenders to me. She goes limp but I have her as she exhales slowly.

I hold her like this for minutes, my lips on her neck, kissing her there. Her arms hold me close across my back and then she takes a deep breath, pulls my head back by my hair, looks into my eyes with passion, and kisses me, "I love you, Shannon," she whispers.

I take a soft terry cloth robe, wrap her in it, guide her back to the bed, and lie beside her. We are facing the window and I am holding her close and kissing her ear and neck. "Look."

I have seen the sun rise over the ocean from this bed hundreds of times; my parents carefully arranged these cottages to take advantage of the sun with the precision of the builders of Stonehenge. I knew by the changing light through the glass bricks of the shower that the timing is flawless.

The sky lightens gleaming off the ocean waves. Indigo slowly becomes yellow at the horizon, followed by radiant orange until the sun itself appears – a bright scarlet orb over blue water shimmering like crystals. Of all the sunrises that I have watched none has ever been as brilliant as this one with Elizabeth in my arms.

Chapter Twenty-Two: Elizabeth

The sun has come up and the room is filled with the early light of day, a slight breeze blows the curtain, I can smell the salt air, and everything is still except for the sound of ocean waves. Shannon lies against my back as close as she can possibly be with her arm around me as she softly kisses my neck and shoulder. Honestly, I could stay exactly as I am right now for the rest of my life.

"I'll make some coffee," she whispers, and I'm aroused simply by the warmth of her breath on my ear.

I am in such a deep state of relaxation and bliss that I couldn't get up for coffee if my life depended on it.

"You can't turn me into a rag doll and then think I can just pop up for coffee or to run errands with you, Shannon."

There is laughter in her voice, and she says, "No one said anything about popping. There shall be no popping in this house. At our age, we could break a hip. Instead let's just slowly extricate ourselves from the arms of Morpheus and leisurely greet the gentle emergence of this new day."

"You are funny. I'm begging you for five more minutes."

"Wish granted," she says but continues to hold me and kiss me. I know that if she goes on like this, I will need more than just five more minutes. I will want all afternoon.

I wonder if anyone else has felt this level of ease with another person. This sense of being held and embraced in the deepest emotional way. I don't know that I've ever felt quite like this before even though I have felt strong affection and attraction for several women. I could never understand why none of those relationships lasted for more than a few years and most of them not even that long.

After I had lived in London for about ten years and at the end of yet another failed relationship, I sought out a therapist who could help me solve the riddle of why lasting intimacy and love always seemed beyond my grasp. I found Dr. Nora Perfect, and she was smart, kind, insightful, and she came into my life at just the right time. She acknowledged that hers might be an unfortunate surname for someone whose work was helping people become whole rather than perfect. She laughed easily and from our first session I felt safe with her and thought she could help me finally find answers.

She was quite a bit older than me, British, had studied in Switzerland at the C.G. Jung Institute and was gentle and intuitive. She sat in an overstuffed chair and I on a couch next to French doors that opened out to a tiny balcony that overlooked a garden. Several bookcases contained artfully arranged volumes. An acoustic guitar rested on a stand in the corner of the room next to a large wooden and uncluttered desk with a stained-glass banker's lamp, a small soapstone figurine of a Laughing Buddha, and an oversized book with a bright red cover that she later told me contained Carl Jung's last writings and drawings. She told me that he had titled this volume Liber Novus but almost everyone today simply refers to it as 'The Red Book.' Original and interesting art hung on the walls and, although there weren't any personal items – like photos of family or friends – somehow this room reflected her. Everything was comfortable and soft and even the ambient lighting was easy on the eyes. I never saw any candles burning but there was a slight scent of vanilla in the air. I am not sure what I expected but this was far less anxiety provoking and more reassuring than whatever I had conjured up.

We spent time discussing my history and, of course, my feelings about Shannon. She wondered if I might be unconsciously doing something to ruin these relationships or, perhaps, I am attracted to the kind of woman who is on the colder end of the temperament scale in the first place. Maybe, like a heat-seeking missile I am always aiming at someone who will never be able to give me what I am so hungry for. As such, my efforts are destined to fail. As I recounted more than just a few of my short-lived relationships I realized that there might be some truth in that. Certainly, that was the case with Lauren all those years ago. We also discussed whether my unrelenting and long-standing crush on Shannon prevented taking a deeper risk with any other woman.

She asked me to pay particular attention to my dreams. "The reason the unconscious is hard to access is precisely because we are unaware of its contents. But these are the feelings, motivators, and urges that operate in our psyche that influence our emotions and behaviors. What is unconscious will be projected and acted out," she told me.

She asked me to imagine an arctic iceberg. She told me that less than a third of the mass of that iceberg is visible above the surface of the water. The rest of it – the vast amount of ice – is deeply submerged. It is not the part of the iceberg that we can see that sinks the ships. What we can see, we can navigate around. She emphasized that it is the part that we can't see that is the most treacherous.

"This is an apt metaphor for consciousness," she said. "Most of what makes up our psyche is beyond our present understanding. Our goal here is to make more of what is unknown brought into the bright light of awareness."

After one particularly emotional session, I remembered a recurring dream that I had from the time I started first grade, and it reappeared regularly though as I got older the repetitions were fewer and farther between. I am on a raft flowing down a river. I am young, maybe still a toddler and I am floating away from the shore as the river starts rolling more quickly. I can see my parents and sister on some kind of dock and I'm calling out to them. They are looking in my direction but are ignoring me or maybe they can't hear or see me. I am starting to panic so I scream louder but they still don't respond. When I first started having this dream – more like a nightmare – I would literally wake up sweating and scared. I only occasionally experience this now and when I awaken from it, I'm no longer terrified. It's still unsettling but not as frightening as it used to be.

We spent several sessions working with these images, and she asked me if I had ever heard about the Mistaken Zygote. I told her that I had not, and she related the story to me.

"In her book called Women Who Run with the Wolves, writer and Jungian analyst Dr. Clarissa Pinkola Estes talks about the idea that she calls the Mistaken Zygote Syndrome. In the beginning you were this fertilized egg and in some other dimension where either a fairy or a big-winged bird puts you in a basket with all the other Zygotes ready to deliver each of them to the families who are destined to raise them. Some of these little potential beings are so excited to be born into the world, to become incarnate that they hop around the basket and accidentally fall out and slip down the smoke hole of the wrong house and a family who was never meant for them and doesn't have a clue as to how to raise them."

She waits a few minutes to let the meaning of this story sink in. "Elizabeth, do you think it is possible you are one of those mistaken zygotes? I know you as a warm, compassionate, open-minded person. Your family, as you describe them, seem quite different in each of those dimensions. Tell me more about that."

I realize that I have never really talked with anyone about my family and, up to this point, I have only said a little about them. Somehow, I always felt disloyal and guilt-ridden if I expressed any criticism because they probably did the best they knew how to do, but if this is one of the things that will help me then I will tell her.

"My family and with the important exception of my grandmother, is cold, judgmental, and unforgiving cloaked in a mantle of obsessive religiosity that borders on the obscene. They have never approved of my life or my choices. They might love me in their own way, but it is obvious that they do not like me. Not in the least and for as long as I can remember."

I know that this conversation is hitting something that is so deep and so ancient for me that it feels like it is baked into my bones. I cried.

With infinite compassion, Dr. Perfect said, "It is no wonder that you have always felt like an outsider with them and, maybe, with others. That dynamic can deliver quite a wound. Is it possible that – at some unconscious level – you don't believe that you deserve the love that you are looking for?"

We sat in silence for the rest of that session while I let that awareness fill my mind.

On another day, Dr. Perfect recommended journaling, basically keeping a diary. She told me that writing thoughts and feelings can be therapeutic and another tool to become a more conscious person. I went to the local bookstore and bought a beautiful handmade leather-bound journal for this purpose. I would sit in front of this imposing volume with its smooth paper and couldn't write a single word. Not one. I was intimidated by just how elegant it was and discovered that I was far more fluent when I used an old composition book that I found in the desk in my home office.

"You write for yourself and your growth," she said, "So don't worry about anything. There is no right or wrong way. Just let your feelings flow."

One of my first entries was on a day when I was feeling particularly lonely and, as they so often did, my thoughts centered on Shannon. I wrote:

One day I will have you.

We will be one hundred years old.

And our bones will crack.

And the passion will turn us to dust.

And it will still have been worth the wait.

I didn't know whether this was a lame attempt at writing a poem or some profound message from the unconscious part of my psyche, but I almost don't remember writing those words. As I thought about them it seemed to me that I was living my life in potential and not reality. I was immersed in a thoroughly fantasized future. Maybe it is true that my strong feelings for Shannon over all these years have prevented me from being emotionally open to any other woman who might love me in the present. Perhaps I have simply been unable to fully engage or to let myself fall in love. I wondered whether or not my lack of finding true love was karmic retribution for the careless way I dealt with relationships – if you even want to call them that – when I was in my twenties. But I haven't been a player like that for a long time.

Maybe my longing for Shannon is some kind of payback for the dismissive and selfish way I handled that morning after all those years ago. Or it is possible that I live in the middle of such a huge abandonment complex that I will never find my way out of it and will always be afraid of emotional risk because I think that I already know the outcome and am certain that it will be painful.

And then there is the widely accepted belief that it is impossible to love another without first loving yourself. Dr. Perfect and I spent considerable time exploring this idea, especially when we considered the dynamics of my family.

"Sometimes we find clear answers and sometimes we are left with simply asking the questions. Remember, Elizabeth, discovering your true Self is the journey of a lifetime. Stay the course, keep writing and honoring your dreams by working with them. When you're on the path…you're at the goal," she said in her quiet and comforting way.

I think that I was making progress in the two years that I had been seeing her when Dr. Perfect told me that she was ill and would be ending her practice in the next few months. She shared that she had a rare type of blood cancer, and that the prognosis was not good. I think that she sensed how upsetting that was, and she reached over and patted my hand. Despite how intimately she knew me this was the first time that we ever physically touched each other. I don't even remember shaking hands when we first met.

She referred me to one of her colleagues who was attached to the same clinic, but we never quite hit it off in the same way. Then my work became increasingly busy with lots of travel, and I saw that new therapist for only a few months before I stopped going.

Dr. Perfect died a month later.

Lying here in Shannon's arms reminds me of just how starved I have been for any touch that is infused with affection and closeness, with something more than just physical desire. I am reflecting on just how loving she is to me. How protective and concerned she has always been for me and how we seem to have a rhythm with each other that defies explanation. We have a true friendship, and it is a beautiful thing. Over the past three days I have felt something changing inside of me. Something that had hardened in ways that I couldn't even describe is melting and emerging. And I wonder if, possibly for the first time, I am allowing myself to not just give but also to receive love.

I wished that on that morning thirty years ago, I had been aware of the things that I learned with Dr. Perfect. I think that I would have been able to see, and to know, immediately the difference between my feelings for Shannon – filled with affection and mutual understanding compared to my relationship with Lauren that was just physical desire and that was all there was to it. I think the only reason I interpreted that as love was because I was so hungry for it. My own emotional illusion. If I knew then what I know now I might not have hesitated for those crucial couple of weeks that changed the ultimate outcome of my relationship with Shannon and for the biggest part of my life.

Time is running out for me to tell her the things that have remained unspoken. Today will be a rush of activities and then we will celebrate Linda. I leave here tomorrow with an early flight on Thursday and unless I gather the courage, I will have lost this opportunity. My hesitation cost me dearly before and I won't let that happen now. I feel my face flush, my heart pound, and an anxiousness overtakes me but, nevertheless, I turn toward Shannon. We are as close as two people can be and I'm desperately hoping that I will not disturb our friendship by what I'm about to say. I'm leaning on my elbow and making direct eye contact with her, and I say, "There's something I need to tell you."

Chapter Twenty-Three: Shannon

I sense the second that everything changes in Elizabeth's demeanor as she turns and faces me. Her body stiffens and she takes a deep breath. She is leaning on her elbow and looks pained as if something big is about to happen or be said.

"Are you okay?"

"I think so. Or I will be."

I reach over and rest my hand on her waist because she looks like she needs some support right now and, I simply can't be this close without touching her.

"I have some things that I need to say about that night all those years ago."

"Okay," I smile and nod, and she takes another deep breath.

"I have never explained anything, and I've wanted to talk about this for years, decades really, but it always felt like this conversation might not be respectful of your relationship with Kim while you were together. In the past year, you've been so involved with Linda and her care that I just couldn't distract you with something that occurred a lifetime ago. And you made it clear that you didn't want to talk to anyone about your relationship with Kim, but I knew you must be devastated. And then there's my resistance – cowardice really – to bringing up our past because I felt so apprehensive and didn't want to do anything to hurt our friendship. So, there has never been a good time…until now. When I have imagined speaking with you about this, I've been nervous because I'm not even sure if or how much you will remember."

"Why don't you try me?"

Elizabeth begins to recount what happened thirty years ago. She tells me about the year-long clandestine affair she had with Lauren Foster. I remember the name and know that she was one of her professors at VCU and a big star on a local news station.

"Lauren Foster, the anchor on WTVR?"

"Yes. She was still living with her husband who was running for public office. Glenn Anderson."

"What? You were seeing the woman who was married to that homophobic, misogynist, racist wanker running for Governor of Virginia against Barry Daniels. That Glenn Anderson?"

"One and the same. But Lauren wasn't like that. She told me that he wasn't either when they first got together but his political ambitions turned him in whatever direction that was most likely to get him elected."

She continues to explain, "She always used her professional name and not her married name. So, their relationship wasn't entirely secret but also not way out there during the campaign because she was in the media and her station broadcast news stories about him all the time. She wanted to keep a low profile as did the television station, to avoid any accusations of conflict-of-interest. It was easier to keep this quiet back then when there wasn't a 24-hour news cycle and everyone in the world wasn't carrying a camera on the cell phone in their pocket."

"Oh God, Elizabeth. That must have been hard for you. Everyone thought he was a total ass and a dangerous one. Almost all of us were volunteering for Barry Daniels."

"On the afternoon that you came over, Lauren had just told me never to contact her again and without any rhyme or reason. I did not know of anything that would make her do that, at least nothing that I was aware of. I only later learned that Glenn was becoming suspicious even though she told me they were separated."

"I'm sorry. That sounds painful and so cruel."

Elizabeth nods in agreement. "I was heartbroken. I raced all over campus and to the tv station but couldn't find her, so I opened a bottle of Tequila. I was well into it when you came by and knocked on my door."

Elizabeth is normally one of the most confident and articulate people I know. But it is easy to see that she is struggling with this conversation. She's nervous and almost stumbling over her words. I move a little closer to her and help with the part of this story that I know.

"It was clear that you were upset about something, and I asked if you were all right and you said, 'not really.' I said that if you want some company, I'm happy to stay for a while. You didn't say a word but motioned for me to sit down at the table and brought another shot glass from that disastrous bookshelf that you built, poured some Tequila for me and another one for yourself and we sat there talking about everything except why you were so sad."

"I think you came by to drop off a book that you had borrowed."

"It was the Clan of the Cave Bear."

"I wasn't sure if you even remembered any of this."

"You were wearing a light-yellow tank top and navy-blue shorts. It was the middle of August and your apartment in the Fan was hotter than the hinges of hell with one, old cranky window air conditioner trying to keep the whole apartment from topping eighty degrees."

Elizabeth seems surprised that I remember all those details. But of course, I do.

She moves closer to me, "I had always been attracted to you even during this love affair with Lauren, but it was a confusing time. You were such a comfortable caring presence to me – just as you always had been. But that night you gave me some refuge when I felt my heart would never recover. The attraction that had always been there and everything about that night conspired to make me want to make love with you. More than anything. And then we split that bottle of Tequila and opened another. Any inhibitions that I ever had disappeared and then I could not take my hands off you."

I had always felt that strong attraction to Elizabeth but since nothing ever happened while we were getting to know each other, I could never be sure that the feelings were mutual. We never went on a date, never kissed, never did anything physical except for what good friends do together.

I explain my perceptions at that time and tell her how I was also confused.

"For the whole year when we were becoming close, I thought that we were communicating something with eye contact and all those subtle signs that signal attraction, but nothing ever came of it. I decided that maybe I imagined that the flirting was mutual. I knew that I was interested in you but was certain that you just didn't feel that same way toward me. Until that night."

She puts her hand on my cheek as if to bring me closer still and says, "My biggest regret – and I am ashamed of it – is that I lied to you and I hurt you. And I am so sorry. That next morning after that most amazing night, you simply wanted to talk about it, but I shut you down. I told you that there was nothing between us beyond our friendship. What we just had was only about sex – and it was great – but it was nothing more than that. That was not true. I felt things for you that I had never felt before. Some deep connection, something that was more than just physical for me and I was terrified. I had just had my heart broken and handed to me in pieces. But that was not a reason to treat you the way I did. There are no excuses. I was selfish and filled with self-pity at your expense. I hope that you forgive me."

I remember that morning and the sadness I felt when it was clear that I had feelings for her that were not returned, but she wouldn't talk about any of it. Making love with her was all that I had fantasized and more. But that morning it became obvious that this strong attraction only went one way, and I knew that I was just not enough for her. I still had no idea about what was going on and why she had been so sad. I did know that I felt rejected, deeply hurt, and left her apartment as quickly as I could.

Elizabeth is worked up and tears are on the edge of her eyes. I am moved to hold her even closer as I smooth a wisp of her hair from her forehead. Every ounce of guilt she has felt is coming through her right now as evidenced by the tears that are now flowing freely.

"There is something ironic, maybe even bizarre that here we are, and it is you who is comforting me for the way in which I profoundly hurt you all those years ago," she says as her voice is overwhelmed with emotion.

"Elizabeth, long-term friendships with any depth need the ongoing progressions of delight and forgiveness, truth and tenderness. Yes, you hurt me, and it took a long time to get past it but your closeness and support in all the time since then meant that I had to forgive you so that I could always hold you in my heart. And keep you in my life. At this point and after all this time, there is nothing that you could ever do to make me not want to be your friend."

She catches her breath and continues with this story that she seems compelled to finish. "I told you to go to grad school and you did. You were gone in a week. It took me almost two more weeks to sort through my feelings and end it with Lauren. Which I did as soon as I realized that she was not who I wanted. I wanted you."

She moves closer to me and whispers, "Do you remember when I came to Princeton to visit about a month after you moved there from Richmond?"

"Certainly. You came for a conference."

"A half-truth. There was a conference that I could have attended but I didn't have to. The real reason I came to Princeton was to see you. I hoped there might be a chance for us. But you had already met Kim and she had moved in with you. This was in record time. None of us even knew you were seeing anyone. Your relationship took all of us by surprise – especially me – though we all know the old joke about what a lesbian brings to her second date."

"A U-Haul. A stereotype, I know, but that time it held true," I answer.

I tell her that when I met Kim, it felt like I fell in love with her. But my heart was hurting too. I really thought that there was something special between us and that night convinced me of it, but it felt like whatever was ignited had no place to go. There was no future for us. I said that you did not appear to be interested in moving beyond anything more than what we just had.

"I agree that it was insane to move in together after only knowing each other for less than a month but Kim's lease was up, and we were spending every night together at my apartment anyway, and it made no sense to keep paying rent in two places. It was the timing. And I thought there was no way forward with you. If her lease hadn't been up, I don't think we would have moved in together quite that quickly. But our relationship worked for a long time…until it didn't."

"I remember meeting you at that craft brewery – maybe the first one I ever heard of – and was so eager to tell you how I felt about you. I don't think I've ever been that anxious before even though I was always comfortable with you, and we had been friends for a year at that point. Then you told me that you were involved with someone, and you really wanted me to meet her. A half hour later Kim walked in and the three of us had a beer together. I never got any further than that in telling you that I had fallen in love with you."

She moves closer to me and puts her arm on my shoulder and for the first time since this conversation began, she seems calmer, more like her normal self.

"Shannon, I've been in love with you for thirty years but have always known that your relationship with Kim was foremost in your life. I have tried to transform my feelings into deepening our friendship. I realized just what a fool I had been – the biggest mistake of my life – when I met Kim, and it was so obvious that the two of you were in love."

I remember exactly the timeframe that she is talking about. Everyone in our Tribe was moving on. I was at Princeton; Linda had moved back to the Jersey Shore for her partnership in an Art Gallery; Caroline was in San Francisco; Marilyn was attending Law School at UVA and Barbara was trying to get pregnant with IVF; Tonya and Cindy were planning their restaurant, and everyone had either left Richmond or was so busy that there didn't seem to be much time for getting together or hanging out like we were able to do earlier in our lives. I remember feeling an unexpected sadness when Elizabeth told all of us that she had applied for and gotten a job at the BBC in London. We were all excited for her, this was a huge professional opportunity and a giant step-up from working at a television station in Richmond, Virginia. But there was something that felt comforting knowing she was somewhat close by – and I hoped would always be there – just a five-hour drive or a forty-five-minute plane ride and without an ocean separating us. I wasn't quite sure why I could not be just unequivocally happy for her, like everyone else was, though I never shared that with anyone.

She tells me that she saw an astrologer in London about ten years after she moved there, and he used a metaphor about water in a saucepan. He told her that the energy between us was enormous and dynamic like water when it is in a full blistering boil. It's hard to manage that level of intensity. So, sometimes, he told her, you must pull the saucepan off the burner and let everything cool down as much as it can.

"And that's what I had to do to make my life work," she said. "I've had to live with the pan on simmer. But I can't keep it there any longer. And I think that's obvious. My time is up to see if there is any way to correct the biggest mistake of my life."

She leans in and kisses me tenderly whispering, "We had a lot to drink that night. I was so afraid that you wouldn't even recall any of it. And if you did remember then maybe you might have discounted it as a one-night stand, or an alcohol infused tryst. My worst fear was that you could never forgive me for the way I hurt you."

"Did you really think that I wouldn't remember?"

"I wasn't sure."

"It would take more than Tequila to make me forget that night, Elizabeth."

Chapter Twenty-Four: Elizabeth

The entire compound is buzzing with everyone taking care of their assignments for the celebration of Linda's life. And there is a lot to do. We are all eager to help, and the flurry of activity strikes me as a testament to just how well-loved Linda was by all who knew her. The Hudson family has lived in LBI for five generations, and they have hundreds of friends and acquaintances. Linda, especially, made her mark on this community with creative programs she developed like teaching art as a means of expression for at-risk kids. Megan said to expect a huge crowd and we are operating under that assumption.

After leaving Shannon's cottage the first person I encounter is Linda's father. Bob Hudson is an enigma. She once told me that he barely earned a high school diploma, yet he was invited to join MENSA after her mother badgered him into taking a standardized IQ test and, much to his dismay, mailed the application. He has worked all his life as a carpenter and has bragged to me and the rest of the Tribe that he has built more than half of the beach cottages on LBI. It is easy to see him as nothing more than a blue-collar guy who likes to drink beer after a long day of work. But those assumptions would miss a lot about this man.

Linda said that her father was one of the most imaginative people she had ever known. More than anyone else, he encouraged her artistic abilities and urged her to follow her own path while her mother worried that she would never be able to support herself as an artist.

Shortly after I arrived Shannon told me that in the past two months, Bob – with the help of Josh, Ryan, and Patty – built a sturdy ramp since Linda often had to use a wheelchair to get in and out of her house. Rough planks of pine, fir, and spruce flawlessly fastened together by rustproof stainless-steel nails provided an easy in and out for her. But that ramp was never really put to much use because less than six weeks later, Linda told us that she was stopping treatment. Today, Bob is putting the finishing touches on easels that will hold some of Linda's paintings that will be displayed here at the Celebration of her life. For this he has chosen exotic and magnificent wood like English Yew, Purpleheart from South America, and Padauk a brilliant orange hardwood from Africa. He has put these together like the fine craftsman that he is, and the different woods play off each other in such exquisite harmony that it is hard to tell where one ends, and another begins.

The Hudson family was ecstatic when Linda moved back from Richmond to co-own an art gallery on the island. Throughout the years that she has lived here, Bob made easels and displays for the shop, and Linda once told me that more than one customer asked about buying the easel before inquiring about purchasing her painting. "Beauty comes in many shapes and configurations. There can be more creativity in a first-rate soup than a second-rate poem or painting." she told me.

I walk over to say hello to Bob. This is the first time I have had a chance to talk with him since I've been here.

"Hi Bob. I'm so sorry and there are no words."

He sets down the polishing tool and embraces me with a bear hug. "Elizabeth, I'm so glad to see you. This is the hardest thing that we've ever had to do. I worry about Martha."

"I can't even imagine losing a child. My heart is breaking about this loss of such a good friend. I'm glad she has support from you, Emily, Josh, the whole O'Connell clan, and all of us."

He smiles but he is sad. He knows this is true. "If there ever was a time in life where 'it takes a village' was the truth then this is it."

He hugs me again and this time I can feel the tears on his cheek which he wipes away quickly with the back of his hand.

"I'll get back to this now," he says as he resumes the polishing that he had been doing.

He has assembled a half dozen of these easels near where we will be showing the short video that I put together. Shannon and Caroline have gone to the gallery to meet Emily and together they will select the paintings that have been Linda's favorites. They will bring back some of the artwork to display. Shannon told me earlier that she wants to include the vivid wave painting that hangs over her fireplace. We are trying to put together all the things that we know would make Linda happy.

I pass by Tonya and Cindy who are in active conversation with Aiyana, Maria, and some of the kitchen staff. The plan is to serve a variety of tapas and small plates. They have been planning the menu ever since Linda told us that she was finished with chemo and the clinical trial that was not working. I think that we have the A Team of innovative food people working on this part of the event. Of course, there will be a variety of wines and there will be lots of champagne – Linda's favorite libation. And chocolate. For years we have known that when they met in art school at VCU Linda and Caroline bonded over the Austrian chocolates that a friend had sent from Europe.

Marilyn, Barbara, and Nadine are setting up tables where we will display some photos of Linda and memorabilia that was important to her like the ratty old Pride sweatshirt that she has worn since 1981 and has seen better days. Bob and Ryan have provided us with several gorgeous wooden frames for this display using the same exotic woods as for the easels. When I suggested that I could go to the local gift shop and easily buy some frames they looked at me like I was a mad woman.

I walk toward the front of the hotel where I am to meet with Tom, Ryan, and Judy about what we need to do to get ready for the presentation of the video that I've prepared. They are already here, and Tom is up on a ladder and installing another bracket.

"Hey, Elizabeth," he is smiling and says, "How many flags do you think we actually need here? What do you think might be excessive?"

"We do not need to pull Elizabeth into our family drama," Megan says. "We want her to come back!"

Judy grabs my hand and says, "Flags are something of a controversial topic here at The O'Connell Guesthouse. Several years ago, Megan went to a hospitality convention and learned that flags are an inexpensive and colorful way to draw attention to your business and she went to town with it."

"No, she went to several towns with it," Ryan interjects.

"Stop!" Megan says. "It has proven to be an excellent way to draw traffic into the Pub and the restaurant and it is more cost-effective than running ads all over the place."

"Yes," Tom adds. "Until we look like the fucking United Nations!"

"There are worse things to aspire to," Megan says. She is laughing, flirty, and having fun with Tom. This flag business is an ongoing discussion of that I am certain.

Ryan tells me that there are always four flags that fly no matter what: The American Flag, the Irish Flag, the Rainbow Flag, and the one showing the O'Connell Guest House logo. In the last several years, the Ukrainian national flag has joined that grouping of "no matter what else is going on flags."

Megan says, "But we are in a sporty area and on the edges of two major markets. So, from New York we have the Jets, Giants, Mets, Yankees, and the Knicks. From Philadelphia we have equal and passionate sports mongering for the Eagles, Phillies, 76ers. And that doesn't even include hockey and, who knows what other teams or events."

Judy is laughing. "We also get quite a few regular guests from Boston, but Tom won't let us hoist the Red Sox flag unless they are the only ones left in the American League playoffs. Because, you know, Tom and his Yankees."

Tom smiles and nods. "Yep."

Megan shows me the additional flags that will be flying today, and I am surprised and moved to tears to see that they all represent paintings by Linda.

"Shannon found a place that did a good job replicating Linda's art and transferred it to cloth," Megan says. "I think Linda would like these."

"I am certain she would love them," I say.

I enjoy the ease that this family has when they are together. There is always a lot of humor, laughter, and they obviously like being with each other. I can sense just how and why Shannon and the O'Connell's so easily embrace all the rest of us. She told me that when she asked her mother if all the Tribe could come for a long holiday weekend her mother responded in a faux Irish accent and simply said, "Darlin' we can always put another potato in the pot."

I'm thinking about Shannon and wish that I had gone with her to the gallery but right now I must make sure that the technology will support showing this video tonight. There is a part of it that no one is expecting. I have not told anyone. Not even Shannon.

Ryan hands the flags he has been holding to Judy and takes the DVD that I have been carrying with me this whole morning. "We are all good. Wait till you see this setup. The weather should be fine, and we'll show your movie outside."

We walk toward the pool and on the grassy area to the side and even from a distance I can see that he has placed a huge screen. It must be twenty-five feet diagonally.

"We've kept this open grassy field for pick up kickball games, dogs catching frisbees, kids playing catch. Mom is talking about adding Pickleball courts, but we all want to make sure it is not a fad before sinking money into it. If we go with Pickleball, we'll have to find some space by the tennis courts because everyone has lobbied to keep this green space just as it is. Not structured. Not pre-determined to be anything in particular. Kind of spontaneous. Like for tonight and it has been the location of more than a few weddings and outdoor parties. There's plenty of room for chairs and we will need a boatload of them."

Tyler nods hello to us as he and some of the staff have begun to place white folding chairs in straight rows and facing the screen.

Ryan puts the DVD into a drive and presses play. The opening credits come up and the audio is on and sounds good. Everything is a go.

"We can stream it from your phone or other device or use this DVD whichever you want."

"We bought the whole entertainment package so that we could show films even in broad daylight and the technology is amazing. They supplied this giant screen that pops up like a tent. A 4K projector, speakers, all the connectors required. Everything. Even by myself, I can put it up in less than 15 minutes. The company brags that they provide everything except the popcorn, but we have that taken care of also!"

"Do you use it a lot?" I ask.

"You bet. For the last two years. This was originally Jack's idea. He read an article about projectors and saw an ad for that company, and it showed kids in a swimming pool and in chairs around it watching a movie in the middle of a bright, sunny day. He thought that could be a good idea for us. And it has been. It more than paid for itself in the first two months. We have kids' movie night every Tuesday in the early evening, and we are swamped. We conducted a little survey asking all of them what they wanted to eat on those nights and there were two unequivocal winners – and by a landslide: An unlimited Taco Bar and an unlimited Ice Cream Bar for dessert."

Suddenly, Phillip and Rafael appear out of nowhere and grab me by the waist.

"Gurl, you have to see this!" Phillip says. He is slightly – maybe a little more than slightly – buzzed. "Sorry. I'm afraid I was one of the Guinea Pigs for the wine tasting checking the food pairings."

Rafael laughs and says, "The rest of us sipped and spit. We were supposed to be tasting and offering feedback. Phillip forgot that part about not slugging down the whole glass."

Phillip takes me by the hand and followed by Ryan and Rafael we walk towards the center of the compound near the swimming pool and the patio bar area.

"You will not fucking believe this! The swimming pool becomes a dance floor! Watch!"

Ryan tells me that Phillip and Rafael came to Megan with an idea. They wanted to resurrect tea dances.

"Tea dances!" Phillip says. They were so popular in the 50's and 60's for gays. Most people don't know that until 1965 it was illegal in New York – that bastion of liberal thinking – to serve an alcoholic beverage to someone who was known to be gay."

Phillip is swaying and Ryan directs him to a chair, but he can't stop talking. "Tea dances were held in the middle of Sunday afternoons and literally served tea. Tea! Fucking Tea! So we were now law-abiding citizens! The idea spread from New York into Provincetown, Miami, Los Angeles, San Francisco and lasted well into the 1990's. I came out at one on Fire Island. They were awesome!"

Ryan continues the story, "We started these a couple of years ago and they have been incredibly successful and not just for LBGTQ folks but for everyone. But I can tell you that tea is rarely, if ever, served. We have some of the best craft cocktails going at these events!"

We are standing at the edge of the swimming pool. Ryan goes over to what looks like some kind of circuit breaker at the edge of the restaurant, punches in a code to unlock it and pushes several buttons.

Slowly but determinedly the bottom of the swimming pool begins to emerge, and it is wooden. Wooden like a dance floor and it rises while the water recedes around all the sides of it. The whole transition is quiet except for the muffled hum of a motor and the sound of the water flowing over the sides of the wooden insert. The whole process takes less than four minutes. The swimming pool has disappeared. And in its place is a hardwood dance floor.

"What the fuck! We like to swim but, even more than that, we love to dance!" Phillip says.

We can see Megan heading toward the grassy area, clipboard in hand, and leading a utility truck that is transporting a baby grand piano, some microphones, speakers, and a small podium.

Ryan laughs, "Look out! When Mom has her clipboard, it means lots of assignments. More than she can even remember!"

"A baby grand piano? Don't you guys have a portable keyboard or something?"

"Miss Jane prefers a baby grand."

I have no idea who Miss Jane is, but she sounds like a perfectionist.

Ryan continues to tell me that the dance floor has been one reason that they have booked quite a few more weddings since its installation. "The father daughter dance wasn't what concerned us," he said. "But weddings can get a little raucous and we wondered how this thing would hold up with a hundred people doing the Chicken Dance or the Macarena or the Electric Slide. But last year we hosted the state competition for Girls Irish Step Dancing, and those boards took a loud and constant beating. We all stood here frozen and terrified – maybe even anticipating a splash – until the last encore. The girls all left the stage and finally, Dad let out a sigh of relief. We all did. 'Bring on Riverdance,' he said. 'we've got this, mates!'"

Ryan smiles at me "That's a two fer. We have a pool and a dance party. All good."

I'm watching this amazing technology, and, at the same time, I can see Shannon and Caroline arrive and they are talking with Bob about setting up Linda's paintings on his easels. All of this is now lost to me. All I can think about is her.

Chapter Twenty-Five: Shannon

Emily, Caroline, and I had an easy time selecting the paintings that we think were Linda's favorites though there are so many that we all love. When I add the wave painting from my cottage, we will have six of her amazing works of art. As we are talking with Bob about how to arrange them, I see Elizabeth by the pool with Ryan and he is showing her how it transforms into a dance floor. He is likely to leave it in that position now. We have about four hours before the crowd will arrive but there is still a lot to do. Pulling myself away from her this morning was almost impossible. I am so physically drawn to her, and I could not stop kissing her, touching her. But the depth of emotion she showed me as she explained what happened all those years ago touched me in a place that no one else ever has. She was so vulnerable, trusting, honest, and sincere in her remorse that I wanted to make love to her all over again and then just hold her until she felt no more sadness about what happened when we were younger.

"Do you agree, Shannon?" Caroline says as she asks me about the order of easels for these paintings and how we want to arrange them. I have not been paying attention, she smiles at me, nods, and I have no question that she knows that I have been staring across the way and at Elizabeth. I don't know who I think we are kidding when I pretend that no one can see what is happening between us.

"You deserve to be happy, Shannon," she says. Emily and Bob don't have a clue what she is talking about, but I do.

As we are setting up the easels, Megan joins us and everyone in the family and on the staff knows that when she has that clipboard there is a lot that still needs to be done.

"We are in good shape," she tells us. "Shannon we just need to get Linda's painting from your cottage here, then we are good to go. The girls have almost all the food prepared and what is not ready now will be soon. The bartenders are prepping, and champagne is chilled to a perfect Linda temp. Ryan and Elizabeth checked out the video and sound. Flawless. We have every staff member ready to arrive in the next two hours. It really will be all hands-on deck tonight. Tyler even hired his sixteen-year-old cousin to help with parking. He's only had his driver's license since July so Yikes! I'm hoping that all goes well! I just want everything to be perfect as we remember Linda." Megan is obviously becoming emotional, and I go to her and embrace her.

"You have done a masterful job in organizing all of this," I tell her as I kiss her cheek.

"You know it is just so hard to say goodbye to such a sweet soul," she says, and, in typical Megan fashion, she starts to tear up. I love that she is so sentimental and often wish I had that ease of emotion, but we are different in that way.

We are all set on the paintings. Megan says go get ready and most of what needs to be done is completed or, at least underway. "Elizabeth said she will bring Linda's wave over here."

I go into my cottage and Elizabeth is taking down the painting from its place over the fireplace. I have not seen her other than across the compound since I left this morning to meet Caroline and go to the gallery. She easily removes it from the hook, turns, and smiles at me.

I wait for her to set it down and then, I can't help myself, I lean right into her open arms and kiss her passionately. "I missed you," I tell her.

"Me, too."

I can't believe that she is here with me in this new way and that simply thinking about her turns me on with such power. Her arms are around me, touching me softly as she pulls me closer. Her lips are on mine. I know that if we go any further, we will be lost for the afternoon.

It is almost witchy in the way that we both move apart at the same time slowly and subtlety.

"I'm going to take a shower," she says. "In the guest bathroom. By myself."

I laugh and kiss her as she walks down the hallway. One kiss after another and I only stop when she goes into the bathroom and closes the door. She is right. We both are and we know what we must do. Get ready and show up.

I finish my shower, get dressed, and go into the great room. Elizabeth might be the most beautiful woman I have ever seen. She is wearing a white linen shirt with collar, black blazer, and slacks and this is something that is so overwhelmingly simple and elegant that I have no words.

She kisses me passionately, and we head to the door. "It's showtime," she says and knows that is a line from "All That Jazz" that I have always liked. She remembers everything we have ever talked about. We better get out of here fast or I will be all over her.

It is still an hour away from the beginning of this Celebration of Life, but flowers have already started arriving even though Linda's obituary asked that donations be made to her program for at-risk kids or the charity of your choice in lieu of flowers. It seems like many people have elected to do both.

The Third Act

Devin the DJ has set up his equipment and I'm certain that Megan has given him a major list of requests and mostly from her. Tunes will be heavy on her favorites but, to be fair, she has a great sense of music across generations and Devin is likely to be grateful for the tips about how to emotionally move a group of people by the sequencing of songs. He has gotten a lot more gigs here since we installed the dance floor and now even small gatherings have discovered how music changes the energy when people congregate together.

As always, Jack and Patty will ask Devin to play Never Gonna Give You Up when he announces that he is going to play something else. They like that song – Rick Astley's one and only hit – so they can say that they rickrolled dozens – probably hundreds – of people. They don't quite get that this is – technically – not a rick roll but they don't care, Devin has fun with it and I'm not about to tell them.

Elizabeth carries the wave painting to the empty easel by the others and sets it in place. Bob is still there making certain that everything is stable. He must have gone home in the interim since he is now wearing a suit and tie. Things are exactly in place as he knows Linda would want them to be.

All the Tribe is already seated in the patio bar, and I go there and find a spot next to Nadine and Caroline. "You, okay?" Caroline says.

"I'm good," I tell her. She squeezes my knee.

This is going to be a hard part of all of this. Because this is goodbye. Goodbye to Linda. We have loved her for thirty years. Unless some of my friends have some spiritual or religious beliefs that I am not aware of we are hard-pressed to find an answer here.

I have always admired and, at the same time, envied my mother's faith and, even, that of the rest of the family. Though these beliefs did not resonate for me. Megan seems to have found solace in the Catholic tradition that we were raised in. But I don't have that. I never have.

Elizabeth comes into the group and I'm not sure if she has edged her way in or if there was an opening to sit next to me but that is what she does. God, we are so out to all our friends. I smile at just how obvious we are and especially because we have been in such denial believing that no one has noticed.

Megan orders champagne for our little group and two waiters come over with generous pours. They are mindful and give Barbara a sparkling cider. I love that Megan and the others stay aware and conscious about what people want.

As we sit and talk people begin arriving. I can see the front of the hotel. Tyler and his guys are parking cars right and left. This is beginning now. All of us get up and welcome friends and neighbors from the community. This is what we discussed, and everyone is rising to the occasion.

I see Dorothy as soon as she arrives. I was hoping but not sure that she would be here. Since when does a Hospice nurse who works with multiple patients show up at a funeral or celebration of life? But I already know that she is such a good person and emotionally connected to Linda and the Hudson family, so I am not surprised. I go over and give her a hug. I introduce her to Elizabeth who is next to me and to Cindy and Tonya who are right there as well.

Staff are going through the crowd offering hors d'oeuvres and champagne. Large cylindrical coolers filled with bottled water, soft drinks, and ice are set near each of the bars and lines are forming for cocktails, beer, and wine.

I am busy saying hello to so many people from the community that I barely notice when Kim arrives.

"Shannon," she says and before I am even aware of it, she is standing right next to me.

"Kim." I do not know what I expected this to be like. We have not seen each other for over a year. I am uncomfortable but not totally freaking out as I thought I would be.

"Shannon, can we talk?" she says.

"Yes. At some other time. I'm sure that this is not the time or place."

Kim continues anyway. "I'm sorry that this is so hard. I hope that you know that I have always loved you and wish we can still be friends…at some point."

I can feel myself being pulled into a discussion that I don't want to have. At least not right now. But I can't help myself. "I don't blame you for falling in love with Allison. I get it. I forgive you for that. I had forgotten what it felt like to fall in love and how powerful that can be. But I am having a harder time accepting that you lied to me for two years. That's where I'm stuck."

"I never lied." Kim starts to say but I stop her. She is lying to me right now. She is gaslighting again.

"Just stop. I have the receipts. Let's find a way to go forward but please never lie to me again. We can talk another time. This is not where this conversation needs to happen."

As we are talking, Elizabeth comes and stands next to me. She doesn't say a word other than, "Hi, Kim, how are you?" But I feel a sense of protection and concern from her.

Then Ryan signals to Elizabeth, she excuses herself, and walks over to him.

"I know this is no longer any of my business," Kim says. "But it is obvious that you and Elizabeth have something going on. I'm happy for you but be careful. She broke your heart all those years ago. I care for Elizabeth. She's always been a good friend, but I don't know if you can trust her. She is something of a player and I don't want you to get hurt again."

I have no idea how she surmised all that has been happening between Elizabeth and me by that almost instantaneous observation of the briefest of interactions. But she has always been prone to making immediate judgments and this time she is right. I shake my head at her. This is unbelievable. Here is this woman who cut me deeper than anyone else ever has giving advice about avoiding heartbreak.

"I don't actually have any words that express just how ironic it is that you are saying this about Elizabeth when you are the one who has been untrustworthy."

"Just be careful," she says.

I change the subject. "Where is Allison?" I ask Kim.

"We are staying at an Airbnb down the road."

"Well, please call her and tell her to come here. We are not in high school. You were friends with Linda for almost thirty years. She would not want us to do anything other than have peace with each other especially today while we have gathered here to celebrate her."

Kim smiles, turns, and walks away. She immediately takes her phone from her pocket and, I assume, begins to text Allison.

I am less upset than I thought I would be when Kim first texted her intention to come today. Perhaps the passage of time or maybe my feelings about Elizabeth seem to have created a layer of protection for me. But as she walks away one thing is clear. I realize that never again will I risk my heart with anyone like I did with her. She proved to me without a doubt that romantic love doesn't endure. Friendships? Yes, absolutely, my friends will go the distance and I will rely on those relationships to get me through the rest of my life. I am aware of the tremendous sexual attraction we have for each other, but I don't quite know what to make of what is happening between Elizabeth and me. I do know that I can't allow it to unsettle our friendship. I don't want to hurt her, but I can't see any other way forward than to go back to that easy relationship that we have had for all these years, the one we knew to be in place before she arrived on Saturday.

Elizabeth comes back from her chat with Ryan and squeezes my hand. "I thought you did very well with that," she says.

"I did tell her I could handle it. Let's see how I do when Allison shows up."

Elizabeth leans toward me and whispers in my ear, "I've got you."

Chapter Twenty-Six: Elizabeth

We are lucky that the weather gods have graced us with an almost perfect night. There is a slight breeze, somewhat overcast skies which has kept the heat to a minimum, and the temperature is in the mid-seventies. By six o'clock we were jammed with people. Many of them know each other as longtime residents of LBI who knew Linda or are close to her family. Megan has done an outstanding job organizing this event with so many moving parts. As Shannon had said earlier, "This is where Megan's bossy tendency shines. She gets everything done and cajoles everyone into doing what they have to." The affection that these sisters have for each other is obvious even in their teasing.

I am talking with Ryan about the timing of showing the video when I see Allison come into the pool area and meet up with Kim. I'm not sure if Shannon saw them or not but, within minutes, they were sitting with some of the other women in our Tribe. Of course, everyone was welcoming and warm. We've learned over the years that we have to withhold judgement about what happens in the relationships of our friends. The only one who has expressed any disdain about the breakup between Kim and Shannon was Marilyn. "I think Shannon deserved to be treated better than she was and I'm not even talking about their split." That's the only negative thing that she ever said and none of the rest of us quite understood it.

Ryan has set up the small podium with a microphone in front of the screen where we will show the video. At 7:30 on the dot, Megan makes an announcement over the loudspeaker that people should grab a beverage, head to the grassy area, and find a seat for a short presentation.

Judy, Ryan, Josh, and Emily are standing to the right of the screen. Emily will give the eulogy for her sister. Her big sister. Linda was fourteen years old when Emily was born. She gave her the nickname: Oops! There was good-natured ribbing, but it was always clear that Linda was the adoring older sister, and, despite the age difference, they were close. Shannon has told me that over the past couple of years Ryan and Judy – ten years their junior – have become good friends with Emily and Josh. It has been clear to me that they are creating their own Tribe and I know it will be helpful for all of them and the Hudson family during the tough days ahead as they adjust to a life without Linda.

Our Tribe has found the way to the last two rows along with the rest of the O'Connell family. Jack and Patty are sitting between Marilyn and Barbara and each woman has an arm around one of the kids. Shannon puts her hand on my back and directs me into a seat near the aisle. Almost as if on cue, the sky seems to darken a little and stars break through the canopy of clouds.

Father Thomas from Saint Peter's Episcopal Church gives a short invocation to begin.

"Linda wanted something from the church because she thought it would help her mom cope with all of this. She also included one of her mother's favorite hymns," Shannon whispers to me.

Miss Jane Weldon – ninety-four years old and the piano teacher who had instructed both Linda and Emily – sits down and begins. Her clear notes break into the silence of four hundred people in various stages of sadness. She is joined by a trio of singers who, Megan told us, are usually part of a Beatles cover band that plays often in the pub. Linda had requested only two songs: Sand and Water by Beth Nielsen Chapman for her and for us and On Eagles' Wings for her mother.

"And he will raise you up on eagle's wings,

Bear you on the breath of dawn,

Make you to shine like the sun,

And hold you in the palm of His hand."

And if that wasn't enough, the breathtaking lyrics of Sand and Water wash all over me and I can feel the passion and honesty of those words down into my bones.

" All alone I came into this world.

All alone I will someday die.

Solid stone is just sand and water, baby.

Sand and water, and a million years gone by."

I am already starting to tear up. I don't have a clue as to how I have made it this far with the range and power of emotions I am experiencing. Shannon looks over at me, smiles sadly, and reaches for my hand. We no longer care to hide whatever this is that is happening between us.

Bob Hudson moves to the microphone and welcomes everyone. Martha stands next to him, and she looks so tiny, so fragile that my heart breaks for her, for all of them, for all of us. He has a handful of index cards, but I don't see him look at any of them. He thanks the O'Connell family and the Guesthouse for giving space to this celebration of the life of Linda. He is struggling but getting through it. He introduces Emily and tells us that she is a second-grade teacher and not used to talking to adults, but she will give it a go.

Emily comes to the microphone. I have never noticed before just how much she favors Linda and how their family resemblance is so plainly clear. She tells us we all know Linda for her creativity and her kindness, but she wants us to know that Linda also was a force to be reckoned with and how she pushed the commissioners of the township of Long Beach Island and the six small towns on it to work together to create programs for kids who are at risk for homelessness, unwanted pregnancies, drug abuse. Kids who felt like they would never belong.

"She was like a dog with a bone and never gave up," Emily tells several funny stories about Linda, some of which we know and some new ones.

"On the day before she lost consciousness, Linda told me to say goodnight, not goodbye. And that was the last thing she said to me and so I will say it to her now Goodnight, Linda. Not goodbye."

The crowd is hushed. Emily leaves the podium. Josh embraces her and Ryan and Judy hug the two of them. It is sweet and moving and I'm thankful that Megan put boxes of Kleenex at the end of each row of seats. I need them now.

Megan takes the stage and introduces the video. "Our friend Elizabeth Matthews has put together a short video to honor Linda as we celebrate this amazing and beloved woman." She leaves as Ryan takes the podium away from the screen. The first credits roll: We honor Linda Hudson for her indomitable spirit, her kindness, her creativity, and her lessons about how to be a lover of life.

I selected Cris Williamson's song Waterfall because the lyrics convey exactly the overflowing love that Linda had for life itself and because it was part of the music of our coming together all those years ago.

"Filling up and spilling over.

An endless waterfall

Filling up and spilling over

Overall"

I have been extremely careful to make each edit, each movement from one image to the next work precisely to the beat of the music. I have used several Ken Burns effects but also found some new ones that I had not seen before. I took a chance, but it is working. It took me longer to make this ten-minute video than many far more complicated documentaries. I knew that it had to be perfect. Shannon is holding my hand tightly as the images go past us: Linda in all her moods, her daring courage, her ridiculous costumes, and her artistic accomplishments. As I watch it, I'm pleased with the results.

The song ends, the images slowly fade to black and except that there are no ending credits it is not clear if this is over yet. But it is not. I had no idea that Linda wanted to do this until she called me shortly after she decided to end her chemotherapy treatments.

The light fades in and on the screen, it is Linda in the last two weeks of her life. She is obviously weak but there is still such an animated life force in her eyes and her expression. She smiles and speaks:

"I know that I didn't want my friends to see me in this shape but, you know me, I'm allowed to change my mind. I've never taken a selfie before but I'm doing it now and I've learned how to make a video on an iPhone. I reached out to Elizabeth because how many Tribes have their own resident filmmaker? Just one of the many ways that we are so lucky. Elizabeth, thank you, my dear friend." She takes a deep breath and looks straight at the camera. "I know some things."

I can see all the Tribe. We are sitting in the same two rows and there is such emotion. Pure sadness and everyone is reaching for a tissue or passing some to the woman next to her.

"Here's what I know. Time flies and there will never be enough of it. We can fight it, we can deny it, we can pretend that we can rise above it. I can tell you that it will claim all of us. That's the bad news. But the good news is that each moment gives us an opportunity, a new chance to be fully alive, to love, to give, to create. Time is capricious. When you are fifteen and waiting for sixteen so you can get your driver's license, time moves at glacial speed. When you are a week out from the onset of a fabulous vacation, the minutes seem like hours, and you think that big day will never arrive. But when you are sixty something or older, you want time to slow down because it is moving too fast. Way too fast. My biggest fear was never about dying. It was always about running out of time."

Shannon squeezes my hand harder. I think this could be one way she discharges her feelings. Almost everyone else in the crowd is wiping tears away. Some, including Caroline, are weeping.

"We can stay stuck in this idea of linear time, or we can find our way into knowing, really knowing, that the only reality is this present moment. This very one. The one we are experiencing right now. Being mindful of exactly this second. Time is not about the future or the past. It is about now. I have learned this. I wished I had known it earlier in my life but, you know, you get it when you get it. More than anything, I have wanted to fully live my life in the world and not just have visited."

Her impassioned feelings are clear to me, and I tried to edit out some of Linda's video that showed how she was tiring since she asked me to do that.

"My beloved family and friends. I honor you. I thank you for giving me the most beautiful life. Emily, you will always be my baby. Josh, my bonus little brother. Please take care of each other. Mom and Dad, no words are necessary except thank you and I love you. Shannon, best friends are made through laughter and tears, and we've had more than a fair share of both, haven't we? To My Tribe – Together we created the container in which we were formed as adults and what a time we had! We have hung together in good times and bad. I will be with you. You have always been my tether, my connection to feeling loved and sheltered. And to Mary Oliver who I hope to meet wherever it is that I am going. I thank you for your poetic wisdom and your words which help everything make sense. Because it is all about staying present and living your wild precious life. Isn't it?"

Doesn't everything die at last, and too soon?

Tell me, what is it you plan to do.

with your one wild and precious life?

There is a pause. Linda looks directly into the camera and with the smile that everyone recognizes she simply says: "I'm talking to you."

Fade to black. It worked and I am so glad to know that the technology and the editing decisions that I made with Linda's approval conveyed what she wanted to say. I'm relieved and take a deep breath. Shannon leans over and kisses me.

"Beautiful," she whispers.

Ryan takes the microphone. "Linda asked specifically that there should be champagne, chocolate, and that, mostly, there must be dancing." This is the cue to Devin to start playing some tunes and the crowd moves to the dance floor and the bars. Champagne is still being delivered throughout by numerous wait staff.

I hold Shannon closely as we dance to slow songs, and I can barely contain myself. I have no idea what is going to happen tomorrow. I will leave in the morning, but I am confident that something powerful has occurred between us and I know that we will find a way forward. Two things are apparent to me. One, everyone on this compound can tell just how we feel about each other, and two I am so profoundly, completely, madly in love with her.

Wednesday – 3 am

Chapter Twenty-Seven: Shannon

It was a beautiful but exhausting evening. The Tribe, Megan, and the crew put together a soulful, honest celebration of Linda's life. Everything from the eulogy that Emily wrote to the moving video that Elizabeth produced and to the words that Linda herself said about how life only really vibrates in the present moment were a testament to her spirit and how she so deeply touched everyone who knew her. Champagne flowed – she would have loved that – and there was dancing. I am certain that if there was anyone who did not sense what was happening between Elizabeth and me over the last few days had no doubt after seeing us dance to slow music. Ryan smiled and shot me the secret hand signal usually reserved for PDA between Megan and Tom that means, "Get a Room!" I pointed this out to Elizabeth and we both laughed. Marilyn came over, put her arms around each of us and kissed us on our cheeks. I guess this was some kind of blessing – if you were being blessed by The Godfather. So, I would say that we're pretty much out now to the family and the Tribe.

The whole event was bittersweet but wonderful in ways that showed just how special Linda was to everyone who had the good luck to know her. There were lots of tears and twice as many laughs. Just as Linda would have liked.

Elizabeth and I have a chemistry and attraction that cannot easily be put into words. There is something so touching about her and connected with feelings that I have never experienced before. Quite simply, she takes my breath away. We made love, closed our eyes in each other's arms, and drifted off into a deep and seemingly dreamless sleep.

Everything was fine. No, it was better than fine. Holding each other was just the right finish to such an emotional and significant day. So, I am puzzled and terrified by what is happening now. Elizabeth's arm is around me and I was sleeping until just a minute ago when I bolted awake, sweating, and trembling. I am lost in a dream, but I am unable to move or scream. I am paralyzed with the dream image closing in on me. I'm sure this is only a matter of minutes, but it feels much longer and as if I will never come out of it. Finally, I gasp for breath and can move my body. I slip out of bed as quietly as I can. I don't want to wake Elizabeth. My legs are shaking, they feel like rubber, and I'm not sure if they will support me over the few steps to the bathroom.

Somehow, I make it there and splash cold water on my face. My fingers are almost numb, and my hands are shaking. I have only had this kind of massive panic attack once before in my life and that was decades ago. I was fifteen and scared to be coming out as a lesbian even though my family is caring and open-minded. I never for even one second thought that they would stop loving me. My mother asked me what was wrong, and I couldn't say. I could only tell her that I felt 'strange' but she seemed to know what to do to help me.

I recognize these same panic symptoms now. My heart is pounding as I try to catch my breath. My fingers are tingling and my whole body feels like it is electrified in a sinister and alarming way. I am hyperventilating and I feel so dizzy that I am afraid that I will pass out. I have to move, or I will jump out of my skin but there is no place to go. I take a deep breath, hold it while counting to five, then slowly release. Can I really remember how my mother helped me through that panic attack all those years ago? I can only recall that she had me focus on my breathing. I throw up, then sit down on the floor and strain to remember the parts of the dream that are still somewhat clear to me.

I am in the middle of a town square or a shopping mall but whatever it is has been closed for the night. There are no cars or people that I can see, and I have no idea how I got there since I don't have any transportation home – wherever that is. I walk up a steep hill and see a road leading into a valley. I sense a woman standing next to me, but I don't know who it is. I feel like it could be Kim or maybe Elizabeth. I turn to ask her if she feels it is safe to proceed down this road, but she has disappeared. I am completely alone in this place. It is snowing now and getting colder by the minute. All the trees are covered with ice and are translucent. The snow comes down at a blinding rate. The only colors are white and silver. I am freezing and I only see a long barren road stretched out in front of me that meanders through this forest of crystal trees. I look both ways hoping to see the headlights of a car or anything that suggests that other people might be nearby, but nothing moves. I look around to see if that woman has returned but she has not. The full moon is my only source of light. I begin to walk down the road and I am by myself and frightened.

Things are moving too fast. I am falling hard for Elizabeth and at the same time I have no faith in attraction, relationships, or anything that looks like a commitment, and I know that is what she wants and has always wanted. She's been more disclosive than she ever has been about her feelings for me and her hopes for the future. We are in very different places. She hungers for what I know is an illusion. I no longer believe that this kind of love endures, and she can't stop believing in it.

I brush my teeth, take a drink of water, and stumble back to the bed. I resist lying close to her, so I keep my distance and hug the edge of the mattress. What was I thinking to get in this deep with Elizabeth? I wasn't thinking at all, only reacting. I know what I have to do, and I can't let myself be pulled into the harbor of her arms, into that magnetic field where I will not be able to, even for a moment, consider ending this.

Elizabeth will be leaving today, and I don't want to hurt her, but I will have to find a way to say that this is where we are now, but we have to go back to the good friends we have always been. I cannot trust that there will ever be anything more than that. She thinks that she has found what she has been looking for in me. But she is wrong. Sadly wrong. And that is the tragic flaw in our story. I am fragile, vulnerable, and so broken. Nothing about love seems to last and I am certain that I cannot take one more loss when that breaking point is inevitably reached with Elizabeth. I can't do this. I can't allow her all the way into my heart that is shattered, and I might already be in too deep. She is a good and loving woman and deserves so much more than what I can give her. I have to make a decision that will protect both of us. I do not know how or even if we can put this genie back in the bottle without sacrificing our friendship, but I must do that. We have to get back to where we once were.

Wednesday – 5:30 am

Chapter Twenty-Eight: Elizabeth

It is just before dawn when I realize that Shannon is not next to me. I get up and look in the bathroom. She's not there. I pull on a robe and walk into the rest of the house. She is not here either but there is a note on the table.

E – Couldn't sleep. Decided to take a walk but back soon. I made coffee but you might need to heat it up. S

This seems bizarre to me. She has not walked on any other morning since I arrived. It is not even fully light out and I would have been happy to go with her if only she had asked.

She's made coffee, the burner is off, but the pot is still warm, so she has not been gone for long. I open the front door where I have a view of most of the beach, but I don't see her there. I pour a cup of coffee and realize that I can't text or call her since her phone is on the kitchen counter. I have no choice but to wait and see what this is about.

I have been up for over an hour and a half. I have double checked email and texts to see if she sent anything earlier about how long she will be gone. But there are no messages from her today. Finally, I take a shower, pack my suitcase, make the bed, and unsuccessfully try to read a magazine that is on the coffee table.

The door opens and Shannon comes in and she looks upset, frozen.

"Are you okay?"

"I'm fine. I just needed some space and a walk seemed like a good idea."

I move toward her and put my hands on her hips, and she almost imperceptibly pulls away. The movement is so subtle that I might have easily overlooked it but during the last several days I intimately understand how her body reacts to my touch and this is something new.

"We need to talk." she says. She sits down on the couch near but not close to me.

"All right but you have already told me that when someone begins a conversation with those words that wherever this is going will be bad news." I am only half joking, but she doesn't smile.

At this point it is abundantly clear to me that the energy between us has shifted to a new – unrecognizable – form. This is not what we have had over the last few days as lovers and not even the familiar one as friends for more than thirty years.

"This is not going to work," she says.

"What is not going to work?"

"This new form of relationship between the two of us. That is what is not going to work."

My heart sinks and I have no understanding about what has occurred in the last six hours to change from such deep affection to this cold standoff.

"We don't have to figure out everything right now," I say with the hope that maybe her reluctance to move forward is logistical. "There is time to work out the rest of it. I want to be with you and if you do, too, then I believe that we can make that happen."

I start to suggest options and emphasize patience about how this could unfold. I say that we can take this real slow. But she immediately explains that it is more than just a problem of distance and geography.

"It is not about the miles that separate us, Elizabeth, it is about what each of us wants in our lives at this time and we are too far apart to find common ground."

"What are you saying? I don't understand. I felt like we had such a connection, even more than we ever had. We've been sad together, laughed, made love, and I felt close to you in every one of those moments. What is going on, Shannon?"

"This time together had been wonderful and a comfort beyond words especially given how much grief has surrounded us. But I'm not ready for what you want. We are good friends, and it should be obvious that there is a strong attraction between us. But what we've had over the past four days is just about sex. Sex and friendship. And, please, don't get me wrong. It has been great, but we want different things."

"How can you be so certain that you know what I want?" I say. I am feeling so many emotions all at once that I can't tell whether I am frustrated and almost angry or so sad that I can hardly find the words to say anything.

"You've made it clear from the beginning. You want a committed, lasting forever, love of your life. You have been looking for your Anam Cara and you mistakenly think that it could be me."

Of course, she is right about what I have been looking for though I haven't said that to her in so many words.

"Why can't we just accept that we are good friends – lifelong friends – and that the past few days were just that boiling saucepan probably spurred on by grief and a host of emotions too many to name."

"That's not what I believe." I was not prepared for this and have no clear answers to what she is bringing up. "I'm in love with you. It is not that complicated. I've known you and loved you for most of my adult life. The last few days have been just a way of opening an expression of these feelings that we had not explored before."

I move toward her and place my hand on her knee but there is no reaction. I am looking directly into her eyes, but she is distant and can't hold eye contact with me.

"Look. I love you. I am not going to hurt you. Ever."

"Oh, please," she says. "I know that you mean that when you say it but, Elizabeth, no one goes into a relationship expecting that they will hurt each other. But they always do. Don't they?"

"You can trust me."

"How can I possibly trust your love? You broke my heart all those years ago and you can't promise that it could not happen again."

That was a deep cut and I almost don't have any response to it. I quietly say, "I thought that I explained that and that you had forgiven me."

"Yes. You explained and, of course, I have forgiven you. But forgiving is not forgetting, and I have to guard what's left of my heart."

Her voice and demeanor became much warmer when she says, "You might not know it at this moment, but this is about me and not you. It's my problem, my fears, my self-protection. I'm afraid that whatever this is between us and any future for me is collateral damage from Kim's betrayal. You are so wonderful in every way, and you deserve a lover without all this sad baggage. I know that someday you will find her. I will be the first one to celebrate with you when that happens."

I do not know if I have any more words that will change anything. I stand up, holding back tears. When I get to the door, I turn, look directly into her eyes, and say, "For the first time and with you it seemed like my life had finally come together. I honestly thought that I had found what I was searching for. But now it is clear that I have seriously misunderstood what has been going on between us. It is not just about sex and friendship for me, Shannon. Not even close. I have such a longing for intimacy without bounds, a hunger to know you on every level and in every way possible. I appreciate your intention, but you don't need to protect me. I can take care of myself."

I pick up my suitcase and continue though I am barely holding it together, "There is such a profound sadness in this moment. Thirty years ago, I let my fear and broken heart prevent anything more between us and now here we are, all this time later, and you are doing the same thing. We can analyze this in all kinds of ways but why should we? The truth is that we don't have another thirty years to get it right. I am in love with you, and it really is just as simple as that."

And then I am out the door.

Wednesday Noon

Chapter Twenty-Nine: Shannon

The look on Elizabeth's face as the door closed and she left the cottage brings me to my knees. She is so hurt, inconsolable, and I am the one who caused it. As soon as those words about not being able to trust her love came out of my mouth, I wished that I could snatch them back. They were cruel and not even true. But I know that I am too fragile right now to risk the possibility of another big loss and my feelings for Elizabeth are coming to a dangerous level. It is far more than I can manage. She does not realize it yet, but I hope that in the future she will. I am incapable of giving her what she needs and deserves. She is a beautiful loving woman and I hope that she will find someone who sees all of that and more in her.

There is no way to move forward from here anyway. The logistics alone are daunting. Her life is in London, mine is here and so long as my mother is alive, that is not going to change. I know that those things could be worked out. But I have no confidence that anything lasts. Certainly not love. That's what I thought I had with Kim only to be betrayed and set aside in this last part of my life. Elizabeth said that the energy between us was like a pot of water in a full boil and she was right. These feelings are so powerful that I am not sure where I can put them in my life. There is really no place for them. And last night, the dream I had and the immense panic attack that followed it shook me to the core. I am still experiencing traces of that and am unsteady on my feet. I'll wait a few days, call Elizabeth in London, and do everything I possibly can to salvage our friendship. I have to be able to do that. Our relationship as friends is an essential part of me and I can't imagine my life without it.

I am trying to get back to some semblance of normalcy after Elizabeth left but I am shaken up and can't seem to figure out what to do next when my phone indicates a text has arrived and it is from Megan.

"Talk?"

"Okay," I text back.

"Come to the house. I will make you a nice cup of tea."

I walk across the compound and Megan is sitting on the front porch. She has already poured the tea and I'm certain she made it before I even responded.

She doesn't waste a minute. I sit down and before I can take the teacup from the table, Megan begins, "Elizabeth came to say goodbye and she didn't want to talk but she looked miserable and upset so I know something happened and I can only guess. Every one of us has always known there was a special friendship between the two of you for all these years and the past few days just confirmed that. I don't want to hurt you, Shannon, but I must tell you something. You are at a crossroads, and you can either stay stuck in your grief or you can open to this woman who has loved you for thirty fucking years. She has always been here for you. Flew in from a shoot for an overnight when Dad died so she could be here for his funeral and to comfort you. She has been here for you and this family since you have known her. She has supported everything you have ever done professionally. She is kind, smart, witty, successful, gorgeous and – above all – she loves you."

I stop her right there, "This is probably too much information, but I think this was just a physical attraction thing, we've always been drawn to each other, but we are friends, and that's it. Think of it as a thirty-year crush that for some reason went a little further this week. And you are right. I do love her, but as friends, we just really have a connection that way like Friends with Benefits."

Megan shakes her head at me. She is incredulous, "Then you have not seen the way she looks at you. Or the way you look at her, for that matter. You might be the only person who has been around here for the last four days who doesn't get what's going on between the two of you. For someone with a Ph.D. from Princeton, honestly, you can be kind of clueless. Shit happens in life, Shannon. And guess what, there's more to come."

Megan gets up and almost stands over me. I don't know if this is her way of conveying older sister power or that she is just so wound up about what she is saying that she can't sit down. She continues: "And I don't mean to go all New Age mindfulnesszen on you, but this present moment is what you've got. It is what we all have. Mom is in her final chapter and we're all in the Third Act ourselves. So, there are going to be a lot more losses. I figured out that if you just live long enough, you will lose everything. But we still have choices. When Judy and Ryan lost their baby in the third trimester they were devastated. The nursery was all set up, they had already named him Sean. They could have said "no" and stopped trying for more children so they would not have to go through that heartache again. But they didn't and because of that we have Jack and Patty. Mom could have closed this business after Dad died but she didn't. Overnight she went from being a teacher to a businesswoman and made O'Connell's into something awesome where lots of people gather to celebrate, make memories, and have fun. You come from a long line of Irish fighters so act like it."

"You're being kind of harsh, aren't you?" I remember all the times we played on this porch as children and Megan was always bossy. She was the teacher when we played "school," I was the student. She was the manager of the supermarket when we played "store," I was the girl who stocked the shelves.

And now she is telling me that she knows what I need to do but she doesn't have any idea, really, about just how terrified I am.

Megan puts down her tea, gets up, reaches over, and takes my hand. "I love you – we all do – we want you to be happy. Don't overthink this, Shannon. You tend to do that. Let your heart lead you and go to her."

Just then, Tom pulls up with the kids in the car and they come running up the steps. They give hugs and I get up to leave. I don't think there is anything more that needs to be said. Megan squeezes my shoulder, and her tone softens significantly, "We love you. And, yes, there will be a lot of difficult and sad things to come, Shannon, but remember, you don't have to go through them alone. You have family and friends who love you deeply. We will do it together."

I collapse on the couch when I get back to my cottage. The range of emotions that are running through me is off the charts. Although she was only here for a few days, everything now reminds me of Elizabeth. The kite she brought for the kids is on the family table, a bit of flour still left on the kitchen counter, the scent of her hair on my pillowcase, the memories of making love with her and the tenderness of her arm around me when we drifted off to sleep.

I go into my office looking for something useful to do to take me away from all these overwhelming feelings. I begin to unpack the small box of my mother's things that they gave us at Northview. Elizabeth had rightly noted that a life – even one well-lived – is, in the end, reduced to just a small number of belongings. Which is why what matters is what you hold in your heart and your memories and in what you leave behind, the love you gave along the way, she had said. She is right.

I put the wedding photo of my parents on the shelf with others of my family and friends. Then I take out the copy of my book that I had signed for my mother just a few years ago. She was so proud of me for writing the stories about so many amazing women. As I am placing it on the bookshelf an envelope falls out. I immediately recognize my mother's handwriting on the short note inside. It is dated a year ago about a week after I told my family that Kim and I were splitting up and just before my mother's almost precipitous decline in her Alzheimer's symptoms. I sit down at my desk and read it.

"My Dear Shannon, I know your heart is broken but please do not be afraid to fall in love again. She might be the love of your life, or she might not be. But please don't let your fear keep you from ever knowing. I love you so much and want you to be happy. Love, Mom."

Megan is right. I have been clueless and the evidence for that is all around me. It is impossible to miss the synchronicity of Pulling the Death Card – and all that it means – when Nadine did the Tarot spread with me, Linda's final instructions to live our one wild and precious life, the truth that Megan just told me, and now this letter from my mother. But the most powerful urges of all are my feelings about Elizabeth and how she unlocked something in me that I thought was gone forever. In a sudden burst of consciousness, a coming of an awareness that has – up to now – eluded me, everything becomes clear. I am in love with her and though I cannot predict anything about the future, I can choose what I will do right now. I will find her and do everything I can to get her back.

Chapter Thirty: Elizabeth

I am having trouble sleeping even though I am exhausted. I have closed the blackout curtains in this hotel room so that I can get some rest, but I can't stop thinking about the last several hours and I'm more confused than ever. I do not know why things changed overnight that dashed all my hopes that Shannon and I could move forward in this relationship. I don't know if I will ever find out.

On the way to my car, I stopped in the lobby to say goodbye to Megan and thank her for all she has done over the past several days. As I expected, she was working at the registration desk and smiled as I approached. Quickly she judged that something was not right, and she came around from behind the counter and gave me a hug.

"Are you okay, Elizabeth?"

"I'm fine," I lied but she was not having it.

"Bullshit you are. What's happened?"

"I think there was a misunderstanding about the changed relationship between Shannon and me."

"I'm so sorry. From my vantage point it looked like you and Shannon were beginning something really good. And for both of you."

I can tell that Megan was open to talking about it, but, honestly, I was out of words. I gave her a hug, thanked her for everything, and told her that I would be in touch.

"We love you, Elizabeth, and I am always here for you. I am only a phone call or text away if you want to talk."

Tyler brought my car around, loaded my suitcase in the back seat when my phone indicated that a text had come in. I was hoping against all odds that it was Shannon saying, come back here and let's talk about this. But the text was from Susan.

URGENT. Plans have changed. Do NOT go to NYC. Flight tomorrow out of Newark is changed due to Zoom meeting conflict. Crew members are in four different time zones and I'm going fucking crazy organizing it. Of course, all this happens when your secretary is on holiday! Just go to Atlantic City. A room at the Borgata is booked for you and you go out of there tomorrow to Philadelphia and then back home. PLEASE CALL OR TEXT AS SOON AS YOU GET THIS so that I know you got it!!!!!!!!!! Plus, I can't wait to hear all the details about you and Shannon. Love, Susan

Nothing seems like it was going to be easy today. I needed to find the entrance to the Parkway going south which I have never done before. Tyler had disappeared back into the parking lot, but I saw Ryan heading into the pub.

I waved and he came over to my car. "Hey Ryan, I am going to Atlantic City instead of New York and I need some directions to get to the entrance to Parkway South."

"No problem," he said. "You surely aren't flying to London out of the tiny Atlantic City airport."

"No. We had to change a Zoom meeting that made the timing of the flight out of New York impossible. So Atlantic City today then to Philadelphia tomorrow and back to London from there."

"Sounds like a pain in the ass unless you like to gamble. Are you okay? You look a little rough," he said.

"I'm fine."

He nodded and smiled but I could tell by his expression that he knew I was lying just like Megan did. It should be evident to everyone who can see me that I am not okay. Not even remotely fine.

He gave me directions to the entrance to the Parkway heading south. "Don't be a stranger, Elizabeth. We all hope you come back here soon."

"Me, too," I said while the whole time wondering if I will ever come back here given what has happened. At that moment I knew that when and if I would return it will not be any time in the near future.

Before I pulled out, I texted Susan.

I have your text. Going to AC – heading there now. I will call you when I arrive. A lot has changed and none of it good. It will help to talk.

Atlantic City is only forty-five miles from O'Connell's, and I knew that I could be there in under an hour. I wanted to call Susan because she is always such a calming influence and good friend. Ever since Kim and Shannon broke up, she has been the major cheerleader encouraging me to take a bolder approach to let Shannon know how I feel.

"What do you have to lose, really?" she has said numerous times.

Apparently, I had more to lose than either of us counted on.

Another text arrived and I only glanced to see if it is from Shannon – hope springs eternal – but it was once again from Susan. She will be as surprised as I am about the sudden change in Shannon's feelings for me. A few times over the course of the last four days, she has texted asking how things are going. Mostly, I just sent a thumbs up but once I did write that "This could be it!" To which she replied, "Yippee!!!"

Bollocks.

I pulled up to the Borgata valet parking at the entrance where a bellhop took my suitcase, and the parking attendant drove the car away.

Things were a blur as I checked in, but Susan had made all the arrangements. The clerk gave me my room key and directed me to the elevators.

This room is quiet and well-appointed. I took a bottle of water from the mini bar, sat down on the bed, and called Susan. She answered immediately.

"Oh, sweetie, what the hell happened?"

I was at a loss to explain because I really don't know. Last night we made love and then fell asleep. Like all the other nights since this began it was wonderful, passionate. There was no space between us as we slept. And then this morning, Shannon was gone. Out for a walk – which she had not done on any other day and when she returned, she was a different woman.

"I couldn't tell you what occurred overnight because I don't have a clue. Everything seemed fine until it wasn't."

"Do you think that she is just so afraid of commitment after Kim hurt her that she is running scared?"

"That is a possibility and she inferred it, but she doesn't seem to want to try to take it slow. She doesn't seem to want to talk about it or go anywhere with it."

It was helpful to talk with Susan and she reminded me that no one can hurt you as deeply as the one you love. She is right.

We talked for about forty minutes and then I was in a sinking spell.

"I love you, Susan. We'll talk more tomorrow. I'm going to shut my phone off because all that I want to do now is sleep from an exhausting week and all the heartache and upset that is today."

She told me to call anytime night or day which I know I can do. Then I took a hot shower, threw on some shorts and a tee shirt, set my phone to Airplane mode, pulled down the covers and got in the bed. For the first time today, I sobbed, and the tears just wouldn't stop.

Chapter Thirty-One: Shannon

I hope I am not too late. When she left Elizabeth was so sad and I can never hurt her like that again. What I said about what she did all those years ago was uncalled for and, worst of all, I used what she had so painfully, so agonizingly told me as a basis for my charge that I couldn't trust her love. I do not think of myself as an unkind person, but that was cruel. I let my own fears lash out in a merciless way and I hope I can catch her before she leaves for London. I will beg her to forgive me even if she cannot understand. I will beg her to forgive me even if she no longer wants to be with me. I have texted her at least half a dozen times with no response. It is not like her to ghost me or be passive aggressive and I don't understand. But I do know that I must see her, talk to her, beg forgiveness for the hurtful things I said. She is a gentle and compassionate person and I do think she will forgive me because that is who she is. But I do not know whether we will have a chance at this relationship.

She told me that she had a ticket to fly out of Newark tomorrow morning, but I know she will stay in the city which is a quick train ride to Penn Station and then a cab to the hotel. And I can get there in two and a half hours, maybe two if the traffic cooperates. In the past she has stayed with Kim and me when she was in town. But before we moved there, she always stayed at the Four Seasons. At least I am counting on that as a starting point. Eight million people live in New York City and my aim is to find the only one that matters right now.

I ask Tyler to please bring my car and as he goes to get it, I race into the Pub looking for anyone in the family and find Ryan first.

"Can you please keep Molly overnight and ask the kids to check in on Hedy before they go to bed?"

"Sure," he says, "Where are you going?"

"I'm going to New York to see if I can make things right with Elizabeth."

"Shannon, she isn't in New York. She went to Atlantic City instead. She wasn't sure how to get on the Parkway going South since she always goes north so she asked me for directions. That's when she said something about the flight out of Newark tomorrow interfering with a virtual meeting, but she can take a puddle jumper out of AC to Philly tomorrow afternoon. Something like that. I'm not going to ask what happened, but she looked upset."

"What happened is that I'm a fool."

Ryan hugs me, "You have never been a fool. I hope you catch her."

The good news is that Atlantic City is less than an hour's drive. The bad news is that I have no idea where she will stay there. When visiting for a few days, some of our other friends would take an afternoon to gamble at one of the casinos in Atlantic City but Elizabeth always declined and preferred to hang out on the beach or the pool with Kim and me.

I head south on the Garden State Parkway and try to call Elizabeth. My call goes straight to voice mail just like all the others today. I must try a new plan to find her. It is now eight o'clock in London, not too late for a phone call. Using hands free, I say, "Call Susan."

Susan answers after just one ring, "Shannon?"

"Hi, I'm sorry to call late but I'm trying to find Elizabeth. I know she went to Atlantic City instead of New York, but I have no idea where she is staying. Do you know?" I can tell by my racing thoughts and the pressured pace of my speech that she must think I am on speed or a bad batch of prescription meds.

Susan is a kind-hearted person and we have been friends since Elizabeth moved to London and they became so close. It has always made me happy that she had someone in her life like Susan since there was no love lost between Elizabeth and her sister Melissa and she is separated from the rest of us by an ocean. I'm certain that Elizabeth has told Susan about this morning and that she will take pity on me and tell me where Elizabeth is.

"Shannon, she's got a room at the Borgata. Her itinerary got totally effed up when some of the film crew had to change a Zoom meeting so the timing of the flight from New York was impossible. She has a ticket to fly to Philadelphia tomorrow, a short layover, and then home to London. But I don't know what room she's in and she is not responding to my texts though she did tell me that she wanted to sleep for the rest of the day."

"Thank you. Thank you." Knowing the hotel at least limits my search because there are nine major casino resorts and an untold number of hotels and motels in Atlantic City.

"I hope you can work this out, Shannon. I think you both need each other and I'm rooting for you."

"Thank you, Susan. I'm rooting for us, too."

"Make it work, luv."

Over the last fifteen miles, I have only been paying attention to keeping this vehicle safely on the road because I am acutely aware of just how distracted I am by the countless emotions that threaten to overwhelm me. I try twice more to call Elizabeth, there is no answer, and I don't even bother to leave a Voice Mail since I've left half a dozen already and texted just as many times.

I pull up to the Valet Parking at the front entrance. The Borgata Hotel, Casino and Spa is an impressive and formidable building, forty-three stories high with twenty-eight hundred rooms. If I were hunting for Marilyn or Tonya, I could simply locate the nearest Craps table and there I would find them. But Elizabeth has always said that the constant noise of casinos gave her headaches.

I race into the lobby headed toward the front desk. I might have cut someone off in line because I'm not paying attention to anything other than finding her. Unusual for me since I am normally overly polite.

A desk clerk approaches, smiling, "Can I help you, ma'am?"

"Yes. I'm looking for a friend, Elizabeth Matthews. Can you tell me if she's here? I know it is probably not possible for you to give me her room number, but can you make a call to her room for me?"

This guy is very nice but simply says, "I'm sorry but it is company policy to not give any information about our guests. I'm sorry."

I want to beg him, but I know nothing I can say will override company policy or his friendly but firm smile. I thank him. But I am determined. I will knock on every one of these twenty-eight hundred fucking doors if I must. And that's when I realize that I might be able to find her.

My hands are shaking when I go to the Find My Phone app, and I plug in Elizabeth's username. I smile as I remember this conversation in my kitchen. "Elizabeth Matthews no spaces." I type in the password Skippy0613. Immediately, the app begins to blink, and a map shows up. Thank you, God. Thank you, Apple. I can see that her phone is in this building but what floor she is on is unclear. I race to a bank of elevators. One is empty; I enter and press the button for the first floor. I get out, but the map shows the phone is above me. Based on what I am seeing, I realize that I can get a better signal when I am on the same floor as her phone. I get back in the elevator and press the button for the second floor. I will find her if I must go through all forty-three floors hoping all the while that no one calls Borgata security to stop this insane woman – not even registered to stay here – who is riding the elevators then going down hallways like a lunatic.

I am on the sixth floor when a text comes in. It is from Elizabeth's number.

E: You are blowing up my phone.

S: Yes.

E: I have something to tell you.

S: Where are you?

E: Atlantic City.

S: Me, too

E: At the Borgata

S: Me, too, what room?

E: 751

S: I'm coming up. That okay?

I am in the elevator while we are exchanging these texts, and I am at her room before she can respond to mine. I knock and she opens the door.

"May I come in?" She nods.

"I know that I hurt you."

She simply says, "Yes."

I can see that she has been crying and she starts to say something, but I interrupt her.

"I want to explain."

"You don't have to," she says.

"Let me try."

I can't contain myself and like an explosion I release all the things I have wanted to say. My words come out in a rush of emotion, and I am closer to tears than I have ever been. I can't lose her.

I have never felt awkward around her before, but I do now. She looks hurt, maybe angry, too. I walk toward her. "I am so sorry for hurting you, Elizabeth. Please forgive me. I am a liar, and I am terrified. Nothing seems to last, and I am petrified to love you like I do. It is not true that what we have had is just about sex for me. I do have such great desire for you, your touch, and feeling your body next to mine, is, honestly, indescribable."

I step closer to her now and I touch her arm. "But I also love the way you hold my mother's hand and the patience you show when you talk to her as if she understands a word you are saying. I love the joy you have with the kids, spending time and teaching them. I love that you make me laugh, and your documentaries are filled with truth, and that you can't cook, and make up passwords that break every rule about making up passwords. Mostly I love the way I feel when I am with you. I don't know what the next years will hold for me, but I do know that I want to spend them with you. I am in love with you. Okay. That is what I came here to tell you. But I interrupted you and I'm sorry to burst in here like this."

She comes to me, places her hands on my face and looks directly into my eyes with profound affection. "I love you. I have loved you since the moment we first met. I will wait for you."

There is no space between us, and I feel enveloped, protected by the love we share. "I believe in you."

She pulls me close and holds me as I weep against her shoulder. I have not cried since the day my father died though I have often felt myself pull back tears: Kim leaving me, watching Linda die, seeing my mother struggle to remember. But right now, I am secure in the refuge of her embrace, safe in the shelter of her arms. She holds me tight while tenderly kissing my tears and I am sobbing for all the losses that have been and all those yet to come.

It is a known fact that it is always darkest before dawn. And if you had never seen a sunrise before, you could not imagine the gentle way that the light coaxes the night and pulls it away from the world. A new day has dawned. This last year has been that dark night of the soul for me, and I never expected that I would find love again, much less one like this... A love that for thirty years has been hidden in plain sight.

Making love is richer, more passionate, and intimate than I ever thought possible. We meld together as one with no pretensions, no masks, nothing to separate us. She knows my weaknesses, my failings, my fears, and still loves me fiercely. I feel joined with her in an ancient and eternal way and know that we belong together. She is my destiny.

Just a few days ago, I told Elizabeth about the ancient Celtic imaginings regarding the deep love and friendship that is Anam Cara: Friends who are attached at their very souls and through all time and space. I did not know then that it would be her love that would ignite a new dawn in me and where I felt alone, I am now in intimacy, where I was afraid, I am now courageous. Like the Phoenix rising from the ashes, I am reborn. This is a new beginning and the passion and love flowing through my veins for her tells me without a doubt that I have found my Anam Cara.

Mid-December – 3 and half months later Epilogue

Chapter Thirty-Two: Epilogue Shannon

It is a rare December day, unseasonably warm as we gather for Friendsgiving the weekend before Christmas. O'Connell's is decorated to the nines for all the holidays and at last count there were dozens of menorahs to celebrate Hanukkah, Kwanzaa candles, Solstice displays, and at least fifteen decorated Christmas trees around the property. Each of the holidays has its own designated flag and, as Tom noted, the front of the hotel looks even more like the fucking United Nations than it ever has. When it comes to December holidays, Megan is not of the "less is more" persuasion.

All of us are here even Caroline and Nadine who cut short their ski vacation in Austria for this first Friendsgiving since the Celebration of Life for Linda. We have vowed that we will have at least one every year and we are already checking dates for next year's event. With all these busy people it takes effort to make it work but as Barbara pointed out, "People have weddings and bar mitzvahs and fifty-year anniversary parties and, with enough notice, those they want there can save the date. This is not rocket science but what it does require is a desire to do it." So far everyone is in with this.

Yesterday, Elizabeth and the kids made four dozen Toll House Chocolate Chip cookies for this gathering and we both laughed as we watched them follow her exacting standards carefully measuring each ingredient and putting it in a separate little bowl. "I don't know whether I'm teaching them that cooking may be an art, but baking is a science, and they need to measure. Or if I am making them somewhat neurotic," she said.

So much has happened in the last three and a half months that it's hard to keep up with everything.

As soon as she was back in London, Elizabeth told Susan and Joe her plans and met with her boss. She told him that she wanted to work remotely for the most part and everyone at the BBC was good with that. Her townhouse was on the market for less than a week when it was sold for the asking price. She lives here with me now but travels to London about a week out of every month staying with Susan and Joe in their guest cottage. Often, I go with her.

We are back in renovation as we are adding a large room that will serve as Elizabeth's office and editing suite. The back of the house is torn up, but the rest of the cottage is livable for the duration and they're making good progress. We're on track to have this up and running by the end of January.

The kids are great. Jack shows real leadership and creativity in his Odyssey of the Mind team, Patty is excelling at soccer, and both made the Honor Roll although Patty's teacher noted that she, "Talks too much." To which Ryan responded, "No shit."

Molly is halfway through the certification to become an official therapy dog though she has been in that role since she was a puppy. To watch the residents of the Memory Unit light up when she enters the room is genuinely moving. She is a natural at this and will soon have the diploma to prove it.

Not much has changed with my mother and someone from the family still visits her every day. Watching her decline is a constant ache in my heart and the sadness I feel is hard to put into words. Emily Dickinson, in her typical economy of language wrote: "There is a pain so utter – it swallows substance up." She is right. This is a long and brutal goodbye for all of us. We have hooked up with some other families going through the same thing and we meet with them every few weeks just for coffee and conversation. It seems to be helping all of us. Megan was right when she said that nothing can prevent the losses that are expected in this part of our lives but, thankfully, no one is alone. We are going through this together.

We all still miss Linda every day and we have started an endowment scholarship fund in her name for Art Majors at VCU in Richmond – her alma mater. Caroline and Nadine have made a generous donation to get us started and we are working on fundraising projects for the future including an annual women's golf tournament.

Emily and Josh along with Ryan and Judy formed an LLC and bought out Linda's partner in the Art Gallery. Linda had pushed for more openings for young artists – specifically the at-risk kids who she was teaching to use art for self-expression. It will be a lot of work and it's not like the four of them don't have enough to do but Emily and her mom are going to work a few days a week in the gallery, they have some excellent candidates to fill out the rest of the schedule, and the others are backing it financially. "This is part of her legacy, and we know she would want it to go on," Emily said.

Dorothy has taken on a few shifts at the Northview Assisted Living Memory Unit. We get to see her a couple of times a week when we visit mom and have built a friendship and, as I get to know her, discover that she is even more amazing than I first thought she was. She has a special relationship with my mother and makes sure she is getting the best care.

And a wedding is being planned. Elizabeth and I are going to get married in March on the Vernal Equinox and a powerful sign of new beginnings. This is the first day of Spring. We don't really feel the need for this, but we want to pay homage to Edie Windsor and all the men and women who fought – and continue to fight – for the right to love who you love. Also, Megan and Susan are planning the whole thing, and they are like two excited – even if a little bossy – mothers of brides. We are going to Hawai'i' for our honeymoon accompanied by Megan and Tom, Susan and Joe. Time to get this whole clan together. We have rented a three-bedroom Airbnb in Maui. While we're there Elizabeth will scout locations for a documentary about the impact of sea level rise on American's most isolated state. I did get a contract for the book about Queen Lili'uokalani. I'm eager to explore the landscapes that inspired this remarkable woman. Elizabeth reached out to her family once this decision to get married was made, but her sister declined the invitation for all of them saying something about loving the sinner but not the sin. But everyone else will be there and neither of us has ever been known to turn down a good party.

Our cottage is humming with activity, friends in the kitchen making the sides while a twenty-five-pound fresh turkey is roasting in the oven. This oven has gotten a lot of use in the last few months and since Elizabeth first inaugurated it with the cookies she made for the kids. Molly is circling the kitchen hoping that a morsel of food will drop her way. Marilyn and Tonya – with Hedy nestled between them and purring like a champ – are cheering on the UVA football team in the match up with Virginia Tech. We are all taking the train to NYC tomorrow to see "Stonewall!" Phillip got the job, and he has front row seats for all of us.

Regardless of the time of year when we hold our Friendsgiving gathering, we know that Barbara will always insist that, as a group, we watch "Love Actually." We have seen that movie so many times that all of us know the lines by heart and are not shy about saying them out loud along with the actors. Still, it is fun and sweet to watch it together and this has become part of our Tribe's tradition, and it is on tap for later this afternoon.

Jack and Patty wanted to buy Christmas presents for Molly and Hedy, so Elizabeth took them to Pet Smart. From the kitchen window, I see her pull up with the kids, they hug her then run to their house. Just seeing her walking toward this cottage – our cottage – makes my heart race. I go out the front door and sit on the porch swing as she comes up the walk. She smiles and slides in next to me. She kisses me and I am filled with the elation that I always feel when her arms are around me.

Every morning, I wake up next to Elizabeth's familiar warmth, as I take her in with all my senses and hold her close. I think about how my life is so different now than just a few months ago. I am struck by the idea that there might be a deeper, more profound meaning of Slan Abhaile or Safe Home. Maybe it is more than just an agreed upon farewell message about traveling mercies. Maybe underlying this common expression there is a universal wish, a longing for a container that holds us, encircles us, and shields us from all the grim realities of living a human life. Get safely home to the house of belonging where you need to be.

I am lucky and have always been surrounded by this loving family and these dearest friends. And this passion for Elizabeth completes my life bringing me to a new level of happiness. When I can be fully awake and resonating in the present moment – paying attention to what is happening right now – I realize how untouched I am by the linear passage of time and enter, if even momentarily, into its eternal dimension. I am far from perfect – not even close – about achieving this state of consciousness in any consistent way, but I am working at it. Each day I try to stop ruminating about the past or worrying about the future. It is not easy but when I can capture even a glimpse of this transcendent and boundless state of mind, I am settled, fearless, and know that we have all the time in the world.

Continue to Recipe…

Afterword

Horseradish Encrusted Grouper

Dear Reader – This is an easy recipe that even I can make flawlessly.

Enjoy! Love, Elizabeth

This recipe was generously given to me by Chef Richard Farmer at Jarrett's Restaurant in Memphis TN. It's delicious! Chef Farmer says it is their most popular entree and, of all the items on their menu, by far the easiest to prepare. So, give it a try!

Two Important Tips

1. Use only extremely fresh fish.
2. Use only Panko Breadcrumbs (these are a Japanese style breadcrumb that are lighter and crunchier than most others). "The dish will not be the same or nearly so good if you don't use this type of breadcrumb."

Ingredients:
- Grouper Filets
- Panko Breadcrumbs

- Prepared Horseradish (8 oz)
- 3 eggs
- Butter
- Salt & Pepper

Preparation: Each serving – 5-6 oz Grouper filet

- Make a mixture of 8 oz jar of prepared horseradish and 3 eggs.
- Dredge the Grouper filets through this mixture and then coat with the Panko breadcrumbs.
- Dust with Salt & Pepper.
- Sautee the Grouper filets in clarified butter (heat butter until it is almost smoking). Brown the fish on one side only then TURN IT and put it in the oven (at 450 degrees) for 4-5 minutes. Serve with the brown, crispy side up.

Serve with

Garlic mashed potatoes and wilted spinach. Chef Farmer plates this entrée by putting the spinach down first covered by the mashers and finally the fish on top. Each bite contains a wonderfully integrated taste. He also starts the meal with a fresh salad with vinaigrette dressing and follows the main course with Creme Brûlée.

Note: We can't be certain, but we think the recipe would also work with other light, white fish such as Flounder or Rockfish.

Wine Pairing Suggestions

Two modestly priced and excellent choices that are a real hit with the Tribe are:

Cupcake Pinot Grigio (Cupcake Vineyards, Livermore, CA) and Sea Glass Sauvignon Blanc (Los Alamos Vineyard, CA).

Acknowledgments

I appreciate all these talented people who gave permission to use small amounts of their amazing work in The Third Act. Their words provide a richness of context and I thank them. Kathleen Brehony

~~~~~~
~~~~~~

Mary Oliver:

"The Summer Day" and "Oxygen" by Mary Oliver

Reprinted by the permission of The Charlotte Sheedy Literary Agency as agent for the author. Copyright © 1990, 2006, 2008, 2017; 2005, 2017 by Mary Oliver with permission of Bill Reichblum.

Dory Previn:

Children of Coincidence

Words and Music by DORY PREVIN

@1976 (Renewed) WC MUSIC CORP.

All Rights Reserved

Used by Permission of ALFRED MUSIC

Beth Nielsen Chapman:

Beth Nielsen Chapman "Sand and Water" from the Album Beth Nielsen Chapman Sand and Water. 1997 released by Reprise Records. Permission granted by Beth Nielsen Chapman. Copyright Beth Nielsen Chapman, All Rights Reserved.

Beau Taplin:

Taplin, Beau, "The Awful Truth" in a collection of poetry and prose entitled Worlds of You. Andrews McMeel Publishing, 2018.

Michael Joncas:

On Eagle's Wings by Michael Joncas (c) 1979, OCP. All rights reserved. Used with permission.

Cris Williamson:

Cris Williamson "Waterfall" from the Album The Changer and the Changed. 1975 released by Olivia Records. Permission granted by Cris Williamson. Copyright Cris Williamson. All Rights Reserved.

Babes of Carytown:

Babes of Carytown (Richmond VA). In the late 1980's there were more than 200 lesbian bars across the United States. Today? There are less than 30. There are numerous reasons for this, and you can explore more here. https://parade.com/living/lesbian-bars, all these years later, Babes of Carytown continues to deliver great food, cold beer, music, dancing, fun, and a safe place for our all of us and our allies. This business was a powerful part of community building at a critical time in LGBTQ+ history and we appreciate using Babes in our story. Thank you to Vicky Hester et al.

The Borgata Resort and Casino:

If you are ever in Atlantic City, NJ, please stay at The Borgata Resort and Casino. It is awesome! https://borgata.mgmresorts.com/en.html

United Airlines:

In real life, United Airlines never actually lost our luggage. In fact, they are an extraordinarily good airline with a terrific safety record and friendly skies.

Additionally, they rarely lose luggage.

Cool Whip

Cool Whip and Strawberry Cool Whip Pie are great! Like Elizabeth thought, it is truly "light and refreshing." We urge all our readers to get the ingredients and make it right away. You can find many recipes for this. Here is one:

https://www.momlovesbaking.com/strawberry-cool-whip-pie/

About the Author

Kathleen Brehony Ph.D. is a clinical psychologist whose passion for her work has led her to examine love and loss and the resounding power of friendships to support us even in life's most difficult moments. She is the author of **Awakening at Midlife** (Riverhead), **Ordinary Grace** (Riverhead), **After the Darkest Hour** (Holt), **Living a Connected Life: Building Relationships that Last a Lifetime** (Holt), and co-author with Karen Jones of **Up the Bestseller List** (Adams), with co-author Robert Gass of **Chanting: Discovering Spirit in Sound** (Broadway) and with Esther Rothblum **Boston Marriages: Romantic but Asexual Relationships Among Contemporary Lesbians** (University of Massachusetts Press).

Kathleen was Host and Associate Producer for a weekly television show **All About Women** (WDBJ Roanoke, VA) and produced and hosted a short-form radio program, **Heartwaves**, that ran throughout North America for years. She has been a guest on hundreds of radio and television shows including the

Today Show, was the subject of an hour-long presentation on **PBS** (CPTV, Connecticut Public Television), and is an excellent public speaker.

The Third Act was borne of Kathleen's feeling that so much of the vibrancy of later life—and the singular sexiness of connecting with someone once you really know who you are—is not being addressed in lesbian romance fiction. In **The Third Act, The Comeback,** and future novels, readers will find connections, intrigue—and happily ever afters —when they check in to the O'Connell's Guesthouse on the Jersey shore.

Kathleen lives on the coast of North Carolina.